Typography
for Desktop
Publishers

Typography
for Desktop
Publishers

BUSINESS ONE IRWIN Desktop Publishing Library

by Mark Hengesbaugh

BUSINESS ONE IRWIN
Homewood, Illinois 60430

We recognize that certain terms in this book are trademarks, and we have made every effort to print these throughout the text with the capitalization and punctuation used by the holder of the trademark.

This publication is designed to provide accurate and authoritative information in regard to the subject matter covered. It is sold with the understanding that neither the author nor the publisher is engaged in rendering legal, accounting, or other professional service. If legal advice or other expert assistance is required, the services of a competent professional person should be sought.

From a Declaration of Principles jointly adopted by a Committee of the American Bar Association and a Committee of Publishers.

Senior editor: Susan Glinert Stevens, Ph.D.
Project editor: Karen Nelson
Production manager: Diane Palmer
Cover Designer: Kay Fulton
Printer: Malloy Lithographing, Inc.

Library of Congress Cataloging-in-Publication Data

Hengesbaugh, Mark.
    Typography for desktop publishers / Mark Hengesbaugh.
      p.   cm.—(BUSINESS ONE IRWIN desktop publishing library)
    Includes index.
    ISBN 1–55623–428–7
    1. Desktop publishing—Style manuals. 2. Printing, Practical—Layout—Data processing. I. Title. II. Series.
Z286.D47H45 1991
686.2′2544536—dc20   90–3643

Printed in the United States of America
3 4 5 6 7 8 9 0 ML 7 6 5 4 3 2

To Jean
For your encouragement and support of my dreams

Acknowledgements

Many thanks go to my wife, Jean Houger Hengesbaugh and to Mr. Bernard Lewis Hengesbaugh and Mrs. Anna Catherine Hengesbaugh for their support and assistance. Special thanks go to my partner in *Design Type Service* of Salt Lake City, Clark Kidman. Thanks to Dr. Susan Glinert Stevens of *BUSINESS ONE IRWIN*, for your unflagging enthusiasm. Thanks to *Ultra Type* of Salt Lake City, for Linotype runout and other kindnesses. Finally, many thanks to those in the past who've taught me about type and about perception.

Contents

read me

Competing for Readership

It may be true that one picture is worth a thousand words, but it takes words to say so. Today we are inundated with printed words. Our mailboxes fill daily with unsolicited advertising. We have heaps of software manuals, trade magazines, newspapers, classic books. . . . No other humans have ever had as much published information available to them. There is no time to peruse it all, and no end to its accumulation. Adding to this predicament, newer and very compelling media, such as film, compete for the time and attention we would otherwise devote to reading.

The infant desktop publishing technology, born of complementary printer and microcomputer advances, came kicking and squealing into this environment. Now, for the price of a good used car, anyone can buy a publishing system, create press-ready copy and have it printed. Desktop publishing popularity adds measurable height to our tottering stacks of as yet unread documents. Literally, we have so much printed information around us now that it's difficult to find the facts when we need them. The problem has shifted from not having enough data, to sorting out that which empowers us in our lives.

Accessible Design

For those intending to desktop publish, here lies both danger and opportunity. Your documents must compete with professionally-designed publications for the attention of a busy reading public. The danger is in creating an uninviting or difficult to read document—the less accessible your message to readers, the less often it will be read. To look on the bright side, a window of opportunity is open to provide fully-laden readers with well organized, easy to read, therefore accessible, printed information.

User-friendly computer software is an accurate parallel to accessible printed documents. Popular icon-based programs anticipate the computer user's tasks, present the necessary tools in an intuitive format and make it easy to choose among them. Similarly, by anticipating readers' needs, a document design can be *reader*-friendly. It can make information access swift by visually organizing and prioritizing it in an easily-read format.

Beyond Sales Hype

It has been said that the difference between a used car salesman and a computer salesman is that the computer salesman doesn't know when he's lying. Computer buyers though, are not blameless. Desktop publishing advertisements tout easy-as-a-click-of-the-mouse professional document design. Hopeful consumers believe this outrageous promise, though if it was made concerning their own particular area of expertise, they'd treat it with the deepest suspicion.

As we all know, possession of a palette of paints does not make an artist. Contrary to the ads, effective design and production of a moderately complex and professional-looking document is often trying and always time consuming. No one who hasn't tried it can imagine the difficulties involved. But who'll buy desktop publishing software or the hardware to run it if the advertising promise is, "This little beauty will increase your work load, deadlines, liabilities, and get you involved in a whole new field beyond your current expertise?"

True, a high level of professional publishing skill sometimes is not an important consideration.

Though such training is helpful, using a desktop publishing system to create memos, internal company product reports or pre-formatted graphs does not require any special knowledge of graphic art.

However, if you want your documents created on the desktop to compete in the marketplace and to reflect favorably upon your company—if you are doing a brochure, business plan, annual report, training manual, book, display advertisement, or business card—then learning the basics of design and typography *is* essential. Today's busy reading public is used to sophisticated, professionally-designed documents.

Necessary Training

It's simple enough to purchase desktop publishing apparatus. It's difficult to gain the expertise required to make that system produce highly-accessible printed information that attracts and influences readers. The novice's tendency is to search the page makeup program's menus for design solutions rather than to use that application's brilliant tools to execute a well-thought out arrangement based upon readers' access to a message. The result is an abundance of user-hostile documents. Communication is obscured rather than clarified by its typographical treatment.

Any industry's tools continually evolve, but the desired results remain the same. Publishing is no exception. Desktop systems are a comprehensive publishing tool, encompassing several traditional craft and professional disciplines: Writing, designing, typography, layout and production. Even publishing industry veterans find it challenging to use desktop systems effectively.

Understandably, those who have arrived at desktop publishing untrained and inexperienced in any aspect of the publishing business have a difficult time coping with the enormous array of choices. It's easy to go astray on typefaces, page sizes and margins—to name just a few ways—because the appropriate selections are seldom obvious.

Training Saves Time

Time constraints also exist. Information that is not distributed in a timely manner often is not useful. Experimenting with document design on a desktop publishing system can easily consume huge blocks of your time, and without proper coaching the results will be uneven. When confronted with the overwhelming number of options in creating a document, you need to be able to quickly narrow them down to the few most appropriate choices.

Obviously then, ownership of a desktop publishing system is not an *unmixed* blessing. How do you use the potential power and control that this technology can deliver?

The good news is that you don't have to be an artist to create effective, interesting and tasteful designs that stimulate readership. It's not a skill that you must be born with and it doesn't require inspiration. And you've already begun to learn. As a seasoned reader you've noticed things that work well in print, such as certain magazine advertisements that *draw* your attention and *invite* you to read them, often despite their content. Though you may know what works when you see it printed, you must find out why it's effective and how to apply that principle to your immediate publishing problems.

Type and Design

When meteorologists look at the sky, they don't see clouds like you and I do. They observe cumulus, stratus or cirrus formations. Weatherpeople have extensive nomenclature for that oddly shaped, fuzzy, white stuff up there that we just label clouds. The word *snow* in the Eskimo language is another well-used example of this phenomenon of semantic distinctions. Eskimos are said to have twenty words for snow. One name is for wet snow, one for wind-blown snow, one for igloo-making snow, and so forth. Similarly, Arab Bedouins have a dozen words for thirst. Therefore, it shouldn't be difficult to understand why people in publishing have hundreds of words for type.

If your education and experience are outside the

publishing industry, you probably have about four words for type: small, big, regular, and fancy. You might not know italic from Italian, that's fine; you've never before had a reason to learn. This book will not make you a type snob, but it will help you make the most effective use of type.

Typography is not just typefaces. Broadly, it is the study of what works well in print. It's a discipline with an enormous body of knowledge accumulated steadily over many centuries of practical experience and observation. It is not an exact science, experimentation is usually necessary. Desktop publishing enables the user to see all the elements of a page together on the computer screen and so can be an excellent tool.

Good typographical design visually organizes, prioritizes and punctuates typeset information in a way that is helpful to the readers' comprehension and gives them a favorable impression of what's written. It subtly directs the readers' eyes through the message from start to finish. It is accomplished with a keen awareness of readers' optical sensitivities and a constant attention to what most people consider details. Anything that deflects attention from the message or inhibits its perception is poor typography. A common example of bad typographical design is drawing readers' concentration away from the words by spotlighting an unusual type style.

Using This Book

The purpose of this book is to instruct the desktop publishing system user on the basics of what works well in document design. It is not an academic discussion, it's a practical compendium. It is hoped that you'll apply this typographical knowledge to your own publishing projects and have well-read, effective documents as a result.

This book is meant to be read through completely so you'll understand the distinctions, priorities, and logical progression involved in publication design. The intention is to start a process of visual and mental articulation so that every time you catch yourself admiring an advertisement or a page from a magazine, for example, you will have a new awareness and understanding of the design principles at work. Each instance will lead to a better understanding of using type effectively.

When creating designs on your desktop system, keep this book nearby for quick reference, perhaps with your software manuals. When you're deciding on the size of your newsletter's margins, for instance, you can pull out this book, go to the Table of Contents and find *Page Design* or look in the Index under *Margins*.

In Summary

■ Today the competition for your potential readers' time is ferocious and the amount of information available to them is vast. Your desktop-created publications will vie for attention with those of professional design.

■ All else being equal, the more interesting to look at, easy to read, and visually well-organized a document is, the more likely it will be read.

■ A desktop publishing system will not design a document for you.

CHAPTER

Measuring and Spacing

To create a document with highly accessible information, inviting design, and easy to read style, you must begin simply, with small things. If you put too little space between the words, they appear to run together. Put in too much wordspacing and the reader's eyes are forced into an uncomfortable hop from word to word. The vertical space between lines of type is equally simple but important to the reader's comfort. In small type, such as the text-size type that you're reading now, the difference between easily read and difficult to read can be measured by, among other things, the space between words and the space between the lines. These spatial differences are tiny units about the size of the point of a sharpened pencil, or the thickness of the wire of an office staple.

To measure such small increments, fractions of an inch are awkward and imprecise, millimeters would make more sense, but type and its environment are measured in units called points and picas.

Printer's Ruler

This means that an essential addition to your desktop publishing system is a line gauge. A *line gauge* is a ruler—the best ones are metal—that is marked in point and pica increments (see Figure 1). Points are about one seventy-second of an inch (.0138"). Two points is approximately the thickness of the wire of a paper clip. Twelve points together are called a pica (pronounced py-ca), and it equals about one-sixth of an inch.

The points and picas system of measurement was adopted in the late 1800's by U.S., Canadian, and British typefounders. It's the publishing industry standard because it's elegantly simple and practical. It has only two increments. The points unit is small enough to measure tiny type sizes in whole numbers, while the pica increments are large enough for longer and wider page measurements.

Almost every important element with which you'll be working—type, column widths, the space between lines of type, the thickness of borders—is specified in points and picas. If you are going to publish, buy a line gauge, life is too short to be multiplying and dividing .0138's of an inch. Think of it as an inexpensive way to improve the quality of your desktop publishing life. Line gauges are available at any North American art supply store.

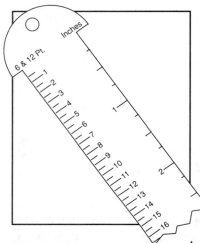

Figure 1. Line gauges measure points and picas and are available at art supply stores.

One nice feature that comes with buying a good metal line gauge—also known as a *pica pole*—is that you can get an amazingly loud bang using only moderate force, from slapping it flat side down on a desk. It sounds like the crack of a large-caliber rifle. This quickly becomes indispensable for venting frustration with a user-hostile computer, for punctuating conversations about deadlines, or for startling sleepy co-workers.

Wordspacing Type

In a perfect desktop publishing world, you would just press your keyboard's spacebar and get the appropriate amount of space between typeset words for that particular situation. This doesn't necessarily happen, and is not likely to be written into the software soon. There are a finite number of factors involved in arriving at suitable wordspacing solutions, but the variety of design environments in which to implement them may be limitless. The ability to know when a computer-generated wordspacing solution doesn't make sense or why it doesn't look good is a uniquely human skill that will always be important and necessary to learn.

Extremes of wordspacing make the printed message difficult to read, so solving the problem of suitable wordspacing is a prerequisite for reader-accommodating design.

Standards for the optimum amount of space between words in typeset material have evolved over the past five centuries that moveable type has been in use. Spacing is based on parts of a variable increment called an em, measured in points. It's named an *em* because it's the same width as the capital M in each point size of type.

Technically, the em is a square, the height and width of which is equal to the point size of type. Practically, the important thing to remember is that an em is as *wide* as the type size is *high*. An em space in ten-point type—ten-point type is what you're reading now—is ten points wide. An em space in 36-point type—represented in Figure 2—is 36 points wide.

An em space is the standard one column paragraph indention for text. (Text is the main body of a printed page, not headlines or captions.) An indention of two full em spaces is standard for text type set more than one column wide.

An em is divided into four subunits: en space, three-em space, four-em space and five-em space. Since an em is the width of the point size of type, these subunits can be calculated as percentages of the point size of type being used.

The regular space between words is the three-em space. The name is a contraction for three-to-the-em, meaning there are three of them in each em (see Figure 2). A three-em space then, is equal to a third

Em space. Unit of measure upon which wordspacing is based.

En space. 50% of type size. Width of figures in most typefaces.

Three-em space. 33% of type size. The regular wordspace.

Four-em space. 25% of type size. Same width as most punctuation.

Five-em space. 20% of point size. Minimum word-spacing on justified lines.

Figure 2. Wordspacing is based on parts of an em. An em's width is equal to type's height in any point size. An em of 36-point type is represented here.

of an em space in width and is about 33 percent of the point size of type being used.

A three-em space is the optimum size of wordspacing to use between words set in lowercase, or capital and lowercase letters. It is a large enough distance between words to keep them from visually running together, but a small enough space so that the reader's eyes are not required to make a distracting jump from word to word. In the wordspacing defaults of your page makeup program, it's very important that you make the setting labeled "desired" the equivalent of a three-em space. More on this later.

Traditionally, the spacing between words of ALL CAPITAL LETTERS is one-half the width of an em space rather than one-third. Words set in all capitals need this extra wordspacing be-

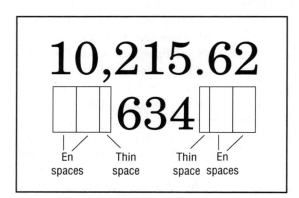

Figure 3. A thin space is the width of many punctuation marks. An en space is equal to the width of the figures in most typefaces.

cause capital letter designs are relatively uniform and blocky. Therefore, when set in all capitals, words are more difficult to distinguish from each other than when they are set in lowercase letters which have more varied sizes and designs. Blocky capital letter shapes give all capitals less space around each letter which also lends itself to extra wordspacing.

Nuts and Thins

The one-half of an em space increment is known as an en space, or a *nut* in the vernacular. It amounts to 50 percent of the point size of type.

In most typeface designs all numbers are the width of an en space. This uniformity ensures that figures will line up with each other when set in tabular columns, such as financial reports or stock market listings.

The four-em space is also known as a *thin* space. Since there are four of them to an em, they are one-quarter of an em in width and 25 percent of the point size of type being used.

By design, most punctuation (, . ; : ') is the same width as a thin space. Having the ability to use both thin spaces and nut spaces on your desktop publishing system is convenient for vertically aligning figures with punctuation without using tabs (see Figure 3). It is also helpful when you want to put hard spacing, or invariable spacing in a line. The space bar will not give you invariable wordspacing in a justified line of type.

When setting type in *justified* columns (see Figure 4), spaces between words vary as necessary to even out the right-hand side margin. A wordspace in justified text though, should be no smaller than one-fifth, or 20 percent, of the size of an em—a five-em space. The maximum wordspacing in a justified line should be no more than an em wide, but it's not always possible to keep it to this limit and a moderate amount of flexibility here is generally acceptable.

Standards of wordspacing for optimum readability have developed over centuries of using type. It's important to check the wordspacing in your desktop publishing system's output against these standard values. No matter how interesting your subject, some of your audience will unconsciously avoid reading what you've written if it is poorly wordspaced.

Chapter Twelve includes step-by-step instructions on how to set your program's wordspacing defaults to these industry standard values.

This type is set on **justified** lines. Both the left and the right margins of each line are evened out by varying the wordspacing and letterspacing within lines.

This type is set on **centered** lines. It has equal spacing between words. No letterspacing is added.

This type is set **flush left.** It has equal spacing between words. No letterspacing is added.

This type is set **flush right.** It has equal spacing between words. No letterspacing is added.

Figure 4. Wordspaces should be the width of a three-em space unless setting justified lines of type or lines of all capitals.

In Summary

- To make a document easy to read, the spacing between words must fall within established parameters.
- The optimum amount of space between words of lowercase letters is 33 percent of the point size of the type being used. For capitals it is 50 percent of the point size of the type used.

CHAPTER

Readability

As you can see, creating a document that's easy to read, therefore inviting to read, starts with basics. Wordspacing thoughtfully, according to publishing industry standards, will enable readers to quickly and effortlessly distinguish one word from the next. Proper wordspacing is essential to accessible design, without it people will resist reading your document.

After appropriate wordspacing come three further indispensable rules for composing a reader-friendly document. The first two are explained in detail in this chapter. The third rule, about typefaces, takes up chapters Three and Four.

Here are the three most important things you can do to ensure that your design is an open door to your message rather than a wall:

1. Set your type in lowercase letters rather than in all capital letters whenever possible.
2. Set text in an appropriate type size and leading for its line length.
3. Use a suitable typeface for the job at hand.

Rule One: Caps

When moveable type was invented five centuries ago, our alphabet had only capital letters. As discussed in chapter One, the blockishness of the design of capital letters and the lack of space around them, make capital letters relatively difficult to differentiate from each other. People read by recognizing the shape of words. When capitals are put together they form words of a uniform, blockish shape, which are challenging to distinguish from each other. Lowercase letters—with more varied sizes and designs than capitals—were invented specifically to make type more easily read.

It follows therefore, that the simplest thing you can do to make your publishing project more readable, is to keep it lowercase as much as possible. This is especially important in text. Text should never be set in all capitals. When it is necessary to set a few words within text in all caps, use SMALL CAPS rather than regular capitals. SMALL CAPS are not as large and clumsy looking as ALL CAPITALS, but they still draw extra attention and so serve the same function.

If you need any more persuasion, consider that using caps and lowercase takes up about a third less space than using all capitals.

Rule Two: A Ratio

Rule two—set text in an appropriate type size and leading for its line length—is a little more complicated than rule one. Here you must consider the ratio between three aspects: type size, space between lines of type, and the length of the line of type.

In typography the word *line* is used only to refer to a line of type—a horizontal sequence of words. Large groups of these lines of type all set in the same way are commonly called columns, as in newspaper columns. A horizontal or vertical drawn mark (▬▬▬ | | |) that in every day language may be called a line, is called a *rule* to avoid confusing it with a line of type.

Leading (pronounced *ledding* to sound like sledding) is the term used to refer to the amount of space between lines of type. Like type's size, leading is measured in points. Leading can be gauged by the total distance from the top of the capitals of one line to the top of the capitals of the next. The word *leading* comes from the metal typesetting procedure of inserting thin strips of lead between rows of handset type to spread the lines out and increase their readability.

Autoleading

If your desktop publishing program has a feature labeled Auto under the leading command, it means that the problem of appropriate leading is automatically taken care of for you, right? Well, no. Autoleading gives an arbitrary leading based on a percentage of the point size of the type selected, commonly one hundred and twenty percent. It does not take into account the type's line length, or the design of the typeface used, or whether the type is a large size or text size. Suitable leading is based on these considerations, so autoleading's usefulness is very limited. It often gives text too little leading, while on lines of larger headline-size type it's nearly always too much leading.

There is more on leading in chapter Three. For now, just remember that leading refers to the space between lines of type.

Line Length

So, when dealing with text in a design, the crux of the problem is the relationship between three aspects of type: point size; amount of words per line, and leading.

Because people read by scanning groups of several words at a time, it requires great concentration to follow small type set across long lines and wide columns (see Figure 5). Without generous spacing between those long lines of small type, it's also difficult for readers to locate the beginning of the following line from the end of the preceding line each time. The more words per line, the more space is required between the lines of type.

The larger the type, the wider a column can be without sacrificing readability. But it's difficult to read large type set on a very narrow column width because it causes sentences to become too fragmented and requires the reader's eyes to shift from line to line too often (see Figure 5).

The idea then, is that a line of type shouldn't have too few or too many words. Some experts say that the optimum number of characters (letters, numbers, and punctuation) per line of type is about

It requires a great deal of concentration to follow small type set across long lines and wide columns. And without generous spacing between those long lines of small type, it's also difficult for readers to locate the beginning of the following line each time. The larger the type size, the wider a column can be without sacrificing readability. The wider the column is in relation to the size of type used, the more space between lines is required. It requires a great deal of concentration to follow small type set across long lines and wide columns. And without generous spacing between those long lines of small type, it's also difficult for readers to locate the beginning of the following line each time. The larger the type size, the wider a column can be without sacrificing readability. The wider the column is in relation

It's also difficult to read large type set on a very narrow column width because it causes sentences to become too frag-

mented and requires the readers to shift from line to line too frequently, both of which are distracting.

Figure 5. The relationship between type size, the length of line upon which it is set, and the space between lines determines whether text is difficult or easy to read.

50 to 60, approximately 8 to 10 words per line. But practically, the best number of words per line for text columns depends upon the kind of publication and its audience.

Newspapers and magazines have relatively narrow column widths, usually about 13 picas—5 or 6 words per line. This enables readers to quickly and easily scan stories that catch their interest. Column widths in books though, are wider—often twice as wide. Here readers have a commitment to absorbing all or most of the contents, and so peruse them with a relatively high degree of concentration, rather than browsing through them. Narrower column widths in a book—creating extra columns per page— would be superfluous.

Words Per Line

Therefore, to give optimum line lengths for point size of type is problematic. More useful though, are minimum and maximum line lengths for each type size. Various typefaces will fit somewhat differently on the same line length though, so remember that the idea is to control the average amount of words per line with your column width, not to slavishly adhere to an arbitrary rule based on numbers.

With that in mind, here's an easy way to remember the narrowest suitable text column width in picas for any point size of type: substitute *picas* for *points* after the type size. For example, the narrowest column width for 10-point type should be 10 picas. The narrowest for six-point type: six picas (see Figure 6).

For type with at least two points of extra space between lines, find the widest suitable text column by doubling the number representing the point size of type you're using and, again, substitute picas for points. For example, if you're using 10-point type, double the 10 and make it picas. So, for readability, the maximum line length of 10-point type is 20 picas. The maximum line length for six-point type would be 12 picas, and so forth.

It is important to apply these maximum column width guidelines to massive areas of type such as columns of text in newsletters and pages of text in books.

Type Size	Minimum Line Length In Picas	Maximum Line Length In Picas
6	6	12
7	7	14
8	8	16
9	9	18
10	10	20
11	11	22
12	12	24
14	14	28

Figure 6. Add one more point of leading to your text type for each 5 pica increase in column width beyond these maximums.

However, a small group of type can be quite readable in much wider lines if it has plenty of leading. The more words on each line, the more space between lines is needed for the reader to be able to comfortably find the start of each subsequent line.

The maximum column width-for-readability rule in Figure 6 assumes leaded type—that's lines of type with two extra points of space between them. If you increase your column width beyond these maximums, add one more point of leading between lines of your text for each five pica increase in column width. For example, if you want to set 10-point type on a column 25 picas wide (five picas longer than the maximum in Figure 6), put at least three extra points of space between the lines instead of the the normal two points of leading between text lines. This means setting your text in 10-point type with 13-point leading rather than 10-point type on 12-point leading.

Narrow Columns

Setting extremely narrow columns not only causes sentences to fragment and causes the reader's eyes to hop from line to line, but it's also a special problem when setting justified text. Narrower columns mean fewer words per line and so fewer wordspaces within which to distribute space to even out the right-hand margin.

The result of setting justified type in extremely narrow columns on desktop publishing programs is very wide wordspaces; too much word division and hyphenation, and wide letterspacing. It makes a line of type look spread out like a picket fence missing a few boards (see Figure 7). Because of these problems, you normally won't want to set your justified type in column widths at the narrow end of the acceptable line length spectrum in Figure 6. Turn your page upside down and you can easily see if the text blocks have rivers of white space running through them, indicating poor type justification.

It can be very appealing to add art (*art* meaning anything on the page that is not type or white space) into text columns and wrap the type around it. However, be especially aware of the minimum column width formula in Figure 6 when indenting text around art—poorly justified lines are especially likely to occur there.

You can also use these minimum and maximum formulas in another way. If you know your text col-

> If your columns are narrow, justified type can be difficult to read because the lines often become noticeably letter-spaced. They also have excessive wordspacing which leaves rivers of white space within the text, and makes some paragraphs look darker than others.

Figure 7. Setting justified columns too narrow for point size of the text type generates badly spaced lines.

umn must be 14 picas wide, for instance, and you want to figure out what point size of type to set the type in, Figure 6 indicates that you shouldn't set it any smaller than 7-point type without extra leading, and no larger than 14-point.

In Summary

- Words typeset in ALL CAPITALS are more difficult to read than words set in lowercase letters.
- Use a moderate amount of words per line of type.
- Adding leading between lines of type enhances readability of text.

CHAPTER 3

Type Nomenclature

Using a suitable kind of type, or typeface, for a publishing project is vital to its readability. Each typeface was created for a certain range of applications. Further, each typeface is designed to provoke its own mental associations from readers by conveying particular characteristics. There are many thousands of useful and beautiful typefaces, but no one of them is fit for every use.

If you use a typeface inappropriately, the type will call attention upon itself and distract readers from concentrating on your message. A very bad choice will make the document laborious to read. By using an appropriate typeface, you will reinforce your message and make it accessible to readers.

Choosing a suitable typeface for a project from among the hundreds available is not as difficult as it might at first seem. It's similar to selecting from among your athletic shoes when dressing for a morning run, rather than from among your dress shoes.

All typefaces are placed within one of six classifications based upon their design characteristics. Each classification is appropriate for some functions and not suitable for others. It's not a question of having to learn the purpose of a thousand different typefaces, it's a matter of learning the characteristics of the half-dozen classifications of typefaces. Learning these basic divisions will enable you to choose from

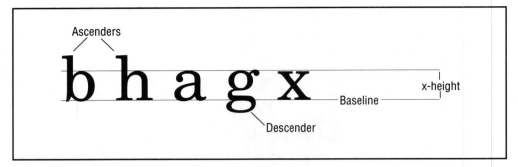

Figure 8.

among typefaces in that classification most likely to solve your immediate design problem.

The components of an individual letter of type—the strokes, the dots and the lines—all have names. In order to properly classify a typeface it's necessary to look at these elements and learn their labels.

Type Anatomy

Letters such as lowercase *b, d, h,* and *l* that have parts that stick up above the mass of the lowercase letters are called *ascending* letters. That part which actually rises up out of those letters is known as an ascender. *Descending* letters, such as lowercase *g, p, q, y,* have portions that fall below the mass of the letters. The part that drops down is the descender (see Figure 8).

In typographical terms, the mass of a letter is known as its *x-height,* because it's most easily measured by the height of the lowercase *x.* The entire height of the lowercase *a,* for example, is the *a*'s x-height while only the upper portion of the *g* is the *g*'s x-height, the lower portion is its descender.

The *baseline* of type is an imaginary line running along the bottom of its x-height (see Figure 8).

Proportional Type

Most typefaces are designed so that the horizontal space that an individual letter is allowed in a line varies in proportion to the shape of the letter. For instance, the lowercase *m* is allowed a wider space than the lowercase *i* because the *m*'s shape takes up more space. Typefaces designed this way are called

Mhijklma
Proportional typeface

Mhijklma
Monospaced typeface

Figure 9. Proportional typefaces have letters that vary in width according to the shape of the letter. Monospaced typefaces allow the same amount of space for each letter.

proportional typefaces. The typeface you're reading, New Century Schoolbook, is a proportional typeface. *Monospaced* typefaces give exactly the same amount of space to wide letters as they do to narrow letters, the same way that a typewriter does. Courier is an example of a monospaced typeface (see Figure 9).

Monospaced typefaces are considered specialty typefaces in typography. They are meant to make a page look as if it was produced on a typewriter. The wide gaps between letters that the non-proportional letter design creates, gives documents a crude look and makes them relatively difficult to read. Non-proportional typefaces also take up much more space for the same amount of words, than do proportional typefaces. These features are not a problem in a memo, but they usually give an unsophisticated look to a document meant for outside audiences.

The *set* of a typeface is the relative wideness or narrowness of the design of its characters. Some proportional typeface designs are relatively more condensed than others (see Figure 10) and this is important because a newsletter's text may fill three and one-half pages when set in one typeface with a relatively narrow set, but will fill four pages when set in another typeface with a wide set.

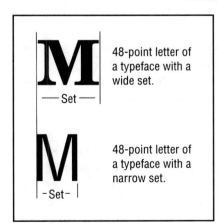

M
— Set —
48-point letter of a typeface with a wide set.

M
- Set- |
48-point letter of a typeface with a narrow set.

Figure 10. The width of a character is its set. Typeface designs vary in their relative widths.

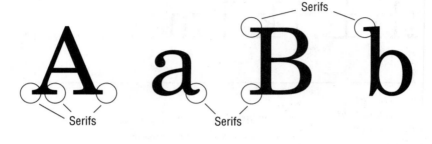

This is an example of a SANS SERIF typeface.

This is an example of a SERIF typeface.

Figure 11. Serifs are the short lines stemming from the upper and lower ends of the main strokes of a letter. They terminate at an angle to the main strokes.

Serifs are the short lines stemming from the upper and lower ends of the main strokes of a letter (see Figure 11). The type you're reading now has serifs. Their shapes can be hooks, blocks, or wedges. They terminate at an angle to the main strokes. Typefaces that have no serifs are called sans serif typefaces, because *sans* means without.

The Face of Type

The part of type that prints—that you can actually see—is the *face*. Faces are the thick and thin strokes, dots and serifs that make up letters and other characters. The face of each letter is designed to align optically with neighboring letters on a common baseline.

The faces of letters are situated upon a space, invisible to users, called the *body* of type (see Figure 12). The height of that body is measured in points and is called the type's point size. For instance, 10-point New Century Schoolbook is 10 points from the top of its body to the bottom of its body.

Type's body goes approximately from the top of the capital letters—or the top of the ascenders—to the bottom of the descenders, but not exactly.

The bodies of most typefaces have extra space built in and this can be measured in large point sizes. For example, the face of 72-point Helvetica measures out to about 69 points from the top of its ascenders and capitals to the bottom of its descenders. The face of 72-point Times is about 66 points high measured the same way. Both are situated on bodies 72 points high and therefore both are 72-point type. The important thing to remember is that you can't measure type from the top of its ascenders or capitals to the bottom of its descenders and come up with the exact point size of that type.

Figure 12. The face of type sits on a body. Point size of type is the height of its body measured in points.

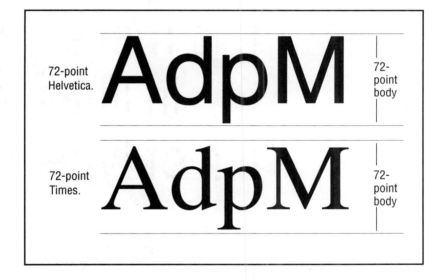

Measuring Leading

You can add to, and reduce the vertical space allowed the face of type, which amounts to adding to, or reducing the space between lines of type. Again, this is called *leading*.

Leading can be measured by the total distance from the baseline of one line of type to the baseline of the next. It can also be measured by the total distance from the top of the capitals of one line to the top of the capitals of the next.

With a line gauge, headline and text leading can

Figure 13. Leading is the space between lines of type and is expressed as the sum of the type's point size and any added space between lines. Shown is 42-point type on 48-point leading.

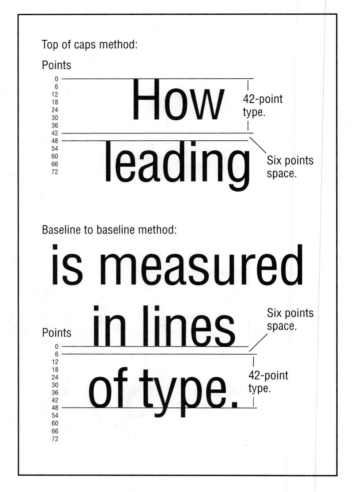

be accurately measured from a sample on a printed page (see Figure 13). When you find an attractively-designed document with a purpose similar to your own project, it is helpful to measure its headline, text and caption leading. This assists you in selecting the leading for the various components of your document.

Leading is not stated as a number expressing only the extra space between lines. It is the point size of type plus any extra space. For instance, 10-point type with three points of space between each line, such as the text you're now reading, is 10-point type with 13-point leading.

In Summary

This chapter's purpose is to familiarize you with type nomenclature so that an advanced discussion of typeface classifications can begin in chapter Four. No need to memorize the terms, if you run into an unfamiliar term in the next chapter, just flip back to chapter Three or look in the Glossary in the back of the book.

■ Typefaces are categorized into a half-dozen classifications. Choosing an appropriate typeface for your immediate needs depends largely upon selecting from the appropriate classification.

CHAPTER

Typeface Classification

Now that you are able to distinguish and label the parts of an individual letter of type, look closely at those elements for their design characteristics. These features reveal a typeface's classification, disclosing an important clue to its successful use.

The designs of typefaces have both functional and aesthetic aspects. When teaching, typographers often over-emphasize the artistic nuances of a typeface. We hear advice enveloped in the obscure language wine connoisseurs use, something like: "It's a naive domestic *Italic* without any breeding, but I think you'll be amused by its presumption," (apologies to James Thurber). Almost as esoteric, here's a quote from a desktop publishing magazine: "This unpretentious typeface shares the qualities of self-effacement and modesty with Zapf 's Melior design while its ruggedness is slightly reminiscent of . . ." But subjective aesthetic evaluations of a particular typeface are unhelpful until long after type users familiarize themselves with the *functions* of the half-dozen classifications of type.

All typefaces within a classification were designed for a certain range of applications. For example, a cursive, or script typeface is the kind of typeface a reader expects to see on a printed invitation. If you choose a typeface from the cursive classification for an invitation, you can't go too far wrong. Some cursives are formal looking, others have a

Zapf Chancery

Diesel Truck Parts

Pretty rugged replacement parts.

STENCIL

AFTER-5

PERFUME

INDUSTRIAL STRENGTH

Figure 14. Typeface selection can be speeded up by eliminating the obviously inappropriate matches of typeface and message.

Roman

Sans Serif

Cursive

Contemporary

Italic

𝕿𝖊𝖝𝖙

Figure 15. Samples of each of the six classifications, or main categories of type.

casual appearance, and choosing among them doesn't require a very subtle or delicate visual palate. However, if you choose a typeface from the cursive classification for pages of text—though it's hard to image anyone who reads making such a selection—it's a serious mistake.

Common sense counts for a great deal in choosing a typeface. For instance, Zapf Chancery is an ornate and elegant typeface. Studying a sample and asking, "For what purpose was this typeface designed?" and "What function do I need this typeface to perform?" will almost certainly lead you to the conclusion that it is inappropriate for use as text and unsuitable for use in a truck parts company's letterhead (see Figure 14). It would look appropriate though, on a formal invitation. You can see by the sample above that the typeface Stencil conveys an industrial or military impression. It, likewise, isn't the typeface to use in a perfume advertisement.

A business with a desktop publishing system is well-served by having an appropriate range of typeface families, not an overwhelming variety. There is no benefit in choosing from among many typefaces with very subtle differences each time you design.

Chapter Six, on design, has more to say about

choosing typefaces, and chapter Ten discusses typeface considerations when printing final, camera-ready pages from a low-resolution output device such as a laser printer.

All of the typefaces mentioned here, as well as those shown on pages 43-57, are available for desktop systems, though some may be available for Apple Macintosh and not for IBM-compatibles.

The Classifications

Typefaces are grouped into classifications according to design characteristics. As previously mentioned, there are six classifications of typefaces—roman, sans serif, cursive, contemporary, italic and text (see Figure 15).

Within these classifications are *families*. A family of typefaces encompasses all the variations in design of a particular typeface. For example: Times, Times Bold, Times Italic, and Times Bold Italic are all members of the same family (see Figure 16). They share the same design characteristics, but differ in weight (or boldness) and slant.

Those variations within families are called *series*. A series is all the variations in point size of a particular style in a typeface family. Times Bold for instance, whether in 6-point or in 96-point, is a series in the Times family.

Desktop publishing mislabels a series *font*. Traditionally, a font is one complete set of type characters, of one size, of one particular series in a typeface family. The distinction is that a font is only one set of one size of type in a series. When you select *font* from the menu bar in a program, you're actually selecting the series of type.

Times

Times Bold

Times Italic

Times Bold Italic

Figure 16. Times is a family of type in the familiar roman classification.

Roman Type

Roman type is the most familiar classification of type to all of us. The text on this page is set in roman type. It's most obviously characterized by serifs and its designs contain much asymmetry to compensate for the optical illusions to which the human eye is prone (see Figure 17).

The readability of roman type has to do with its

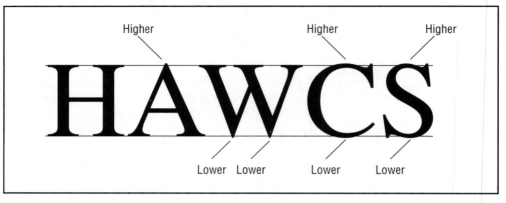

Figure 17. The designs of characters in roman type are intentionally irregular.

familiarity, the space around the strokes, the weight of the strokes, and with its serifs. The serifs provide a visual alignment of the characters in a line of type, so they are excellent typefaces to use for long passages of text. Roman typefaces in fact, are the best text typefaces.

Oldstyle, modern and transitional are the three categories of roman type. These divisions don't depend upon the century within which the typefaces were designed, but upon their design characteristics. For example Times, an oldstyle typeface, was designed in the 1930's. Bodoni, a modern typeface, was designed in the late 1700's.

Type in the *oldstyle* category of roman is rounded at the junction of the serif and the main stem, forming a curved wedge-like bracket (see Figures 18 and 19). It generally has small contrast in the weight of its strokes, meaning that the body of its individual letters are not very thick in some parts and very thin in others. Main stroke angles and the rounded serif bracket angles harmonize in smooth curves. Ascender stroke endings, such as the top of the *l* and the top of the *h*, emulate the graceful angular cut of a letter drawn with a quill pen.

Times
An **oldstyle** roman typeface.

New Baskerville
A **transitional** roman typeface.

Bodoni
A **modern** roman typeface.

Figure 18. Examples of the three categories of roman type.

E l h e

An **oldstyle** roman typeface.

Rounded, wedge-like serifs. Little contrast in the weight of strokes. Angular stroke endings on *l* and *h*.

E l h e

A **transitional** roman typeface.

Less curved serifs. Some contrast between thick and thin strokes. Less angular stroke endings.

E l h e

A **modern** roman typeface.

Squared serifs. Both thick and thin strokes. Vertical stroke orientation.

Figure 19. The design differences between oldstyle, transitional, and modern roman faces.

Because of these characteristics, a page set in text-size oldstyle type has an evenness of tone (sometimes called typographical color) that is described as mellow because it does not dazzle the eye with contrasts. Roman oldstyle type is easily read and does not require much leading because its generally small x-height gives it built-in space between lines.

Generally, oldstyle typefaces look especially good on soft, colored paper and on textured paper. Times, Goudy and Garamond (see pages 43-45) are examples of roman oldstyle typefaces.

Modern roman typefaces have sharp, straight serifs that depart from their main strokes at a ninety degree angle, forming square corners. They have high contrast between thick and thin strokes and have open counters—large enclosed, or partially enclosed, spaces such as the top part of the *e*. They are crisp and finely detailed, giving them great clarity and legibility. Their stroke orientation is mainly vertical. Modern faces express mechanical precision, formality, and authority as opposed to grace and friendliness.

Because of these features, modern typefaces need generous margins and deep leading. For instance, the traditional leading guideline for the modern roman typeface Bodoni is to give it leading equal to its point size plus one-third. That means 12-point Bodoni should go on at least 18-point leading.

Simplicity of overall design is also important when using modern typefaces. Flowery or even curvaceous borders, clip art or ornaments appear tacky in association with their clean, no nonsense designs.

Since modern roman typefaces are more open, they have a wider set. Therefore, they require more space for the same amount of words than transitional and oldstyle typefaces, which are slightly more condensed by design. Of course, if you have a small amount of type to go into a large space, these modern typeface requirements: wide margins and deep leading, are a blessing.

Modern typefaces, of which Bodoni and Impressium are examples, look best printed on hard, glossy paper.

Transitional roman typefaces have some aspects of both oldstyle and modern typefaces, bridging the two categories (see Figure 19). Transitional typeface serifs are less curved than are oldstyle faces and tend towards right angles. Their strokes have more pronounced contrast between thick and thin. Transitional typefaces attempt to obtain the clarity of modern typefaces and the overall readable tone of oldstyle typefaces.

New Baskerville and New Century Schoolbook are examples of transitional typefaces (see pages 46-47).

Sans Serif Type

Sans serif typefaces are the second most-used classification of type. The name points out their most notable common feature: they have no serifs. Lack of serifs generally removes them from consideration for setting long columns or pages of text-size type.

Helvetica

Freestyle

Brush

Times Italic

𝕿𝖊𝖝𝖙

Figure 21.

But sans serif type is fitting for many uses. Its designs are usually simple, orderly and geometric giving it a contemporary look. Because sans serifs are direct and forceful, they are outstanding when used in display advertisements, and as headlines and captions in publications.

Helvetica is a sans serif typeface family (see Figure 21) and may be the most often used typeface family in North America. A complete Helvetica typeface package consists of Black (Heavy), Bold, Book and Light; and Black Condensed, Bold Condensed, Book Condensed and Light Condensed. Because of its great variety of weights and the availability of condensed, it is one of the most practical typeface families to acquire.

Cursive Typefaces

Cursive, or script typefaces are designed to emulate human handwriting or calligraphy. They are graceful and usually elegant. Some can connote femininity, while others, such as Freestyle and Brush, convey an informal friendliness (see Figure 21). Cursive typefaces are especially appropriate for invitations and announcements.

Fancy, ornate typefaces are attractive for a dozen widely spaced lines in an invitation, or a dozen words in a advertisement's headline, but they will stop readers short if used in a paragraph or in small sizes. Also, don't use cursive typefaces in all capitals, they're much too hard to read that way. In fact, use as few capitals as possible with cursives.

Italic Typefaces

Italic typefaces, though considered a separate classification, are still part of the roman, sans serif and contemporary families from which they are designed. They are meant to lighten the formality, mo-

Figure 20.

SETTING ITALIC TYPE IN ALL CAPITALS MAKES IT HARDER TO READ notony and stiffness of upright typefaces. Though excellent for emphasis, they are more difficult to read than roman typefaces and so shouldn't be used extensively as text type.

Within text, use italic for emphasis; for titles of books, newspapers and magazines, and for unfamiliar foreign words and phrases.

Avoid the use of all capitals with italic—this makes it too hard to read (see Figure 20).

Text Classification

When monks copied books by hand before the invention of movable type, the highly ornate quill pen lettering that made up the body of a page was known as text lettering. When moveable type was invented, the first designs were modeled after this elaborate style and so were called text type (see Figure 21). The name of the classification makes it easy to confuse with text-*size* type—that relatively small type used for the main body of a page today.

Using a typeface from the text classification within its special limits is not easy. Text type is challenging to read, even in large sizes. It looks very tacky on cheap printing such as flyers, but it can be used when associated with traditional church publications or holiday cards.

Avoid letterspacing type within the text classification, and unless your audience is composed of cryptographers, don't use text type in all caps—it's just too hard to decipher.

Contemporary Type

Contemporary typefaces are relatively new, as yet uncategorized typefaces and so they have a great variety of characteristics.

Palatino (see Figure 22), one of the most popular contemporary typefaces, has emphatic serifs, delicate bracketing and a chiseled, calligraphic look. It's both elegant in display size and readable in long passages of text.

Lubalin Graph (see Figure 22) is a useful contemporary typeface. It is a square serif typeface, also known as slab serif. This serif design doesn't work too well for extensive text, but the design is good for headlines and captions of less formal documents and for presentation graphics—slides and overheads.

Optima (see Figure 22) is another very handy contemporary typeface. Though at first glance it looks like a sans serif typeface, on closer inspection very slight serifs can be seen. Optima is especially useful for those times when you need a practical, tasteful typeface that holds up well on often-copied documents, such as business forms. Optima is especially convenient to own along with Helvetica for this purpose, not to use together, but as alternatives to each other.

Mixing Typefaces

If you've ever seen someone wearing a striped shirt and plaid pants, you know that clothes can clash. Different styles of typefaces too, can be brought together inappropriately. The basic considerations involved in using different typefaces together are not difficult and if you can learn to choose fitting necktie-shirt combinations for yourself or your spouse, you can select suitable typeface combinations.

Typefaces that go well together are ones that resemble each other in design or tone. All of the typefaces within one typeface family have the same characteristics of design and tone, so you can't go wrong using them together. In fact, it's usually best to use only one family of typeface throughout a publication. Use the full range of the different series within that family. For example, use a typeface family's boldface or black in large sizes for headlines, light italic or bold in smaller sizes for captions, and book (the regular weight) for text.

If you use two typeface families together in the same publication, pick typefaces from *different* classifications. This normally means using a roman type for text—roman is the best type for large amounts of text—and sans serif for headlines.

Using three typeface families in the same publication is not recommended. The extra contrast of a third typeface family's design nearly always brings on a cluttered and unorganized appearance.

Palatino

Lubalin

Graph

Optima

Figure 22.

Design and Tone

When mixing typefaces from different classifications, pick typeface families that harmonize in design and tone. For example, use a wide open, rounded typeface such as New Century Schoolbook for text and a sans serif typeface design with many circular shapes for headlines, such as Avant Garde (see page 51). Another often-seen example is Times for text, which is slightly condensed, and somewhat vertically oriented, with headlines set in Helvetica, which has the same characteristics.

Using Helvetica for headlines with New Century Schoolbook for text in the same document though, is no visual disaster. Both typefaces are suited to the purpose for which you are using them. While they may not especially harmonize, neither do they clash.

Some Don'ts

Using two different families of serif typefaces in a document is difficult to do well because their designs often clash. Combining oldstyle roman typefaces and modern roman typefaces, because their forms and serif styles are different, is not considered appropriate. Using condensed and expanded typeface designs together looks goofy because they obviously disagree in shape.

Note the typeface combinations used in publication designs that impress you. Identify those typeface combinations and find similar pairs in your own collection for your designs.

In choosing a typeface, consider the other shapes in your publication. Judge whether the typeface is appropriate to the shape of the page. Narrow typefaces such as Optima and Garamond (see page 45) can look good on relatively narrow pages but faces with a wide set, such as Palatino, look best with wide margins, not shoe-horned into narrow pages. Faces with a width between wide and narrow, such as Times and New Baskerville (see page 47), can look good on a page of almost any shape.

When using a border with type, select one that goes well with the shape of the type. Typefaces with lots of curves—such as Goudy (see page 44) with its rounded serifs—look good with curved borders. Helvetica, with its straight lines, calls for a straight border. Bodoni with its thick and thin strokes looks good with a border of thick and thin lines.

Typeface Collection

As desktop publishing equipment has proliferated, we see particular typefaces over and over again. However, if you follow the guidelines in chapters One and Two on wordspacing, the use of all capitals, and the line length to type size and leading ratio, it will give your designs a wholly different look than the ordinary document produced on a desktop publishing system. To the reader, even an often-seen typeface will look fresh and inviting when used with generous leading on a comfortable line length.

We now have access to scores of excellent typefaces for desktop publishing systems. Readability, good taste and design elegance though, do not depend on owning many different typeface families. If your business publishes only its own material—even if there is a great variety in it—a well-chosen collection of about a dozen typeface families, in full point sizes from 6-point to 120-point, is quite adequate to the task. Here is a suggested typeface collection with which a business may start. These typefaces are shown on pages 43-57.

Roman Typefaces

Oldstyle. Times is one of the standard typefaces for newspapers, which depend upon readability. Times is excellent for text, and in bold it also works well for headlines and captions. It's a typeface you can use for many purposes—newsletters, memos, charts and graphs.

The oldstyle roman faces Goudy and Garamond are excellent typefaces for business-related documents, especially legal, banking and insurance industry publications. Both are excellent for text, headlines, captions, business cards and letterhead. However, don't mix Goudy and Garamond in the same document.

Transitional. New Century Schoolbook is a very

readable typeface for text and its italic is especially elegant. New Baskerville is also an excellent text typeface and looks good in headlines and captions. *Modern.* None recommended.

Sans Serif Typefaces

Helvetica is a useful all-purpose typeface. Purchase a Helvetica package of Black, Bold, Book and Light, and Black Condensed, Bold Condensed, Book Condensed, and Light Condensed. This variety of weights and widths give it great versatility. Helvetica will work for memos, charts, display advertisements, business forms, flyers, and for headlines and captions in newsletters.

Avant Garde is a modern typeface with geometric lines. It's excellent for display advertisements, headlines, captions and it works well for business forms, flyers and announcements.

Franklin Gothic is an extremely legible typeface with a relatively narrow set. It holds up well on frequently-copied documents such as a business forms. Franklin Gothic also works well for headlines, captions, pullout quotes, charts and business forms.

Cursive Typefaces

Zapf Chancery is an elegant typeface for formal invitations. Brush and Freestyle are script faces that work well for informal invitations, announcements and flyers.

Italic Typefaces

All the listed roman and sans serif typefaces come with italic (or oblique). Also, from the recommended typefaces below, Palatino, Optima, Lubalin Graph and Souvenir come with italic.

Contemporary Typefaces

Palatino looks elegant in large headline sizes and is readable in long passages of text. Use it for business cards, letterhead, display advertisements and flyers.

Optima, like Helvetica, will work for memos, charts and graphs, display advertisements, business forms, headlines, captions and flyers.

Lubalin Graph is a modern, geometric, slab serif

typeface for flyers, informal announcements, head-lines, captions and display advertisements.

Souvenir, with its rounded serifs and unusual shapes, is interesting in display size and readable in text size. You can use it for a broad spectrum of applications needing an informal look.

Text Classification: None recommended.

In Summary

- When choosing a typeface, select on the basis of the function you want it to perform.
- Use oldstyle and transitional roman typefaces to set large amounts of text.
- Using type from three typeface families in one publication is usually too many.

Times Bold. Times is one of the stan
Times Bold Italic. Times is one of the

Times Bold. Newspapers depend upon readability and Times is one of the standard typefaces in journalism. Times is excellent for text, and in bold it also works for headlines and

This is Times in 10-point with 12-point leading. Newspapers depend upon readability and Times is one of the standard typefaces in journalism. Times is excellent for text, and in bold it also works for headlines and captions. It's an all around typeface, you can use it for memos, charts and graphs. Newspapers depend upon readability and Times is one of the standard typefaces in journalism. Times is excellent for text, and in bold it also works for headlines and captions. It's an all around typeface, you can use it for memos, charts and graphs.

This is Times Italic in 10-point with 12-point leading. Newspapers depend upon readability and Times is one of the standard typefaces in journalism. Times is excellent for text, and in bold it also works for headlines and captions. It's an all around typeface, you can use it for memos, charts and graphs. Newspapers depend upon readability and Times is one of the standard typefaces in journalism. Times is excellent for text, and in bold it also works for headlines and captions. It's an all around typeface, you can use it for memos, charts and graphs.

This is Times Bold in 10-point with 12-point leading. Newspapers depend upon readability and Times is one of the standard typefaces in journalism. Times is excellent for text, and in bold it also works for headlines and captions. It's an all around typeface, you can use it for memos, charts and graphs. Newspapers depend upon readability and Times is one of the standard typefaces in journalism. Times is excellent for text, and in bold it also works for headlines and captions. It's an all around typeface, you can use it for

This is Times Bold Italic in 10-point with 12-point leading. Newspapers depend upon readability and Times is one of the standard typefaces in journalism. Times is excellent for text, and in bold it also works for headlines and captions. It's an all around typeface, you can use it for memos, charts and graphs. Newspapers depend upon readability and Times is one of the standard typefaces in journalism. Times is excellent for text, and in bold it also works for headlines and captions. It's an all around typeface, you can use it for memos, charts and

Goudy Bold. Goudy is an excellent t
Goudy Bold Italic. Goudy is an excell

Goudy Bold. Goudy is excellent for many business-related documents. It's an oldstyle design that's extremely readable in text size and graceful in large sizes. Use it for text, headlines,

This is Goudy in 10-point on 12-point leading. Goudy is excellent for many business-related documents. It's an oldstyle design that's extremely readable in text size and graceful in large sizes. Use it for text, headlines, captions, business cards and letterhead. This is Goudy in ten point on twelve leading. Goudy is excellent for many business-related documents. It's an oldstyle design that's extremely readable in text size and graceful in large sizes. Use it for text, headlines, captions, business cards and letterhead. This is Goudy in ten point on twel

This is Goudy Italic in 10-point on 12-point leading. Goudy is excellent for many business-related documents. It's an oldstyle design that's extremely readable in text size and graceful in large sizes. Use it for text, headlines, captions, business cards and letterhead. This is Goudy in ten point on twelve leading. Goudy is excellent for many business-related documents. It's an oldstyle design that's extremely readable in text size and graceful in large sizes. Use it for text, headlines, captions, business cards and letterhead. This is Goudy Italic in ten point on twelve leading. Goudy is excellent for many business-

This is Goudy in 10-point on 12-point leading. Goudy is excellent for many business-related documents. It's an oldstyle design that's extremely readable in text size and graceful in large sizes. Use it for text, headlines, captions, business cards and letterhead. This is Goudy in ten point on twelve leading. Goudy is excellent for many business-related documents. It's an oldstyle design that's extremely readable in text size and graceful in large sizes. Use it for text, headlines, captions, business cards and letterhead.

This is Goudy in 10-point on 12-point leading. Goudy is excellent for many business-related documents. It's an oldstyle design that's extremely readable in text size and graceful in large sizes. Use it for text, headlines, captions, business cards and letterhead. This is Goudy in ten point on twelve leading. Goudy is excellent for many business-related documents. It's an oldstyle design that's extremely readable in text size and graceful in large sizes. Use it for text, headlines, captions, business cards and letterhead.

Garamond Bold in 24-point size
Garamond Bold Italic in 24-poin

Garamond Bold in 18-point. Use Garamond for business documents, especially legal, banking and insurance industry publications. Because it is an

This is Garamond in 10-point on 12-point leading. Use Garamond for business documents, especially legal, banking and insurance industry publications. Since it's an oldstyle roman typeface, it's excellent for text. Use it also for headlines, captions, business cards and letterhead. Use Garamond for business documents, especially legal, banking and insurance industry publications. Since it's an oldstyle typeface, it's excellent for text, headlines, captions and letterhead. This is Garamond in ten point on twelve leading.

This is Garamond Italic in 10-point on 12-point leading. Use Garamond for business documents, especially legal, banking and insurance industry publications. Since it's an oldstyle roman typeface, it's excellent for text. Use it also for headlines, captions, business cards and letterhead. Use Garamond for business documents, especially legal, banking and insurance industry publications. Since it's an oldstyle typeface, it's excellent for text, headlines, captions and letterhead. This is Garamond in ten point on twelve leading.

This is Garamond Bold in 10-point on 12-point leading. Use Garamond for business documents, especially legal, banking and insurance industry publications. Since it's an oldstyle roman typeface, it's excellent for text. Use it also for headlines, captions, business cards and letterhead. Use Garamond for business documents, especially legal, banking and insurance industry publications. Since it's an oldstyle typeface, it's excellent for text, headlines, captions and letterhead.

This is Garamond Bold Italic in 10-point on 12-point leading. Use Garamond for business documents, especially legal, banking and insurance industry publications. Since it's an oldstyle roman typeface, it's excellent for text. Use it also for headlines, captions, business cards and letterhead. Use Garamond for business documents, especially legal, banking and insurance industry publications. Since it's an oldstyle typeface, it's excellent for text, headlines, captions

New Century Schoolbook in t
New Century Schoolboook in t

New Century Schoolbook Bold in 18-point. It is a transitional roman typeface which is easily readable for text and has especially elegant italic.

This is New Century Schoolbook in 10-point on 12-point leading. New Century Schoolbook is a transitional roman typeface which is easily readable for text and has especially elegant italic. Because of its open design and solid lines, it holds up well when reproduced. New Century Schoolbook is a transitional roman typeface which is easily readable for text and has especially elegant italic. Because of its open design and solid lines, it holds up well when reproduced. New Century

This is New Century Schoolbook Italic. New Century Schoolbook is a transitional roman typeface which is easily readable for text and has especially elegant italic. Because of its open design and solid lines, it holds up well when reproduced. New Century Schoolbook is a transitional roman typeface which is easily readable for text and has especially elegant italic. Because of its open design and solid lines, it holds up well when reproduced. This is New Century Schoolbook Italic. New Cen

This is New Century Schoolbook Bold in 10-point on 12-point leading. New Century Schoolbook, a transitional roman typeface, is easily readable for text and has especially elegant italic. Because of its open design and solid lines, it holds up well when reproduced. New Century Schoolbook is a transitional roman typeface which is easily readable for text and has especially elegant italic. Because of its open design and

This is New Century Schoolbook Bold Italic in 10-point on 12-point leading. New Century Schoolbook is a transitional roman typeface which is easily readable for text and has especially elegant italic. Because of its open design and solid lines, it holds up well when reproduced. New Century Schoolbook is a transitional roman typeface which is easily readable for text and has especially elegant italic. Because of its open design

New Baskerville Bold in 24-point siz
New Baskerville Bold Italic in 24-poi

New Baskerville is a transitional roman typeface, more delicate than New Century Schoolbook, and very graceful. It too can be used for text, headlines and captions. New

This is New Baskerville in 10-point on 12-point leading. New Baskerville is a transitional roman typeface, more delicate than New Century Schoolbook, and very graceful. It too can be used for text, headlines and captions. New Baskerville is a transitional roman typeface, more delicate than New Century Schoolbook, and very graceful. It too can be used for text, headlines and captions. New Baskerville is a transitional roman typeface, more delicate than New Century Schoolbook, and very graceful. It too can be used for

This is New Baskerville Italic in 10-point on 12-point leading. New Baskerville is a transitional roman typeface, more delicate than New Century Schoolbook, but also very graceful. It too can be used for text, headlines and captions. New Baskerville is a transitional roman typeface, more delicate than New Century Schoolbook, but also very graceful. It too can be used for text, headlines and captions. New Baskerville is a transitional roman typeface, more delicate than New Century Schoolbook, but also very graceful. It too can be used for text, headlines and captions. New Baskerville

This is New Baskerville Bold in 10-point on 12-point leading. New Baskerville is a transitional roman typeface, more delicate than New Century Schoolbook, but also very graceful. It too can be used for text, headlines and captions. New Baskerville is a transitional roman typeface, more delicate than New Century Schoolbook, This is New Baskerville Bold in ten point on twelve leading. New Baskerville is a transitional roman typeface, more delicate than New Century Schoolbook, but also very graceful.

This is New Baskerville Bold Italic in 10-point on 12-point leading. New Baskerville is a transitional roman typeface, more delicate than New Century Schoolbook, but also very graceful. It too can be used for text, headlines and captions. New Baskerville is a transitional roman typeface, more delicate than New Century Schoolbook, but also very graceful. It too can be used for text, headlines and captions. New Baskerville is a transitional roman typeface, more delicate than New Century School

Helvetica Bold in 24-point size. H

Helvetica Bold Italic in 24-point s

Helvetica Bold in 18-point. Helvetica is a very useful all-round typeface. Purchase a complete Helvetica package of Black, Bold and Book, and Black Condensed, Bold

This is Helvetica in 10-point on 12-point leading. Helvetica is a very useful all-round sans serif typeface. Purchase a complete Helvetica package of Black, Bold and Book, and Black Condensed, Bold Condensed and Book Condensed. The variety of weights and widths gives you great versatility. Helvetica will work for memos, captions in graphs, display advertisements, business forms, flyers, and for headlines and captions. This is Helvetica in ten point on twelve leading. Helvetica is a very useful all-round sans

This is Helvetica Italic in 10-point on 12-point leading. Helvetica is a very useful all-round sans serif typeface. Purchase a complete Helvetica package of Black, Bold and Book, and Black Condensed, Bold Condensed and Book Condensed. The variety of weights and widths gives you great versatility. Helvetica will work for memos, graphs, display advertisements, business forms, flyers, and for headlines and captions in newsletters. Helvetica is a very useful all-round sans serif type

This is Helvetica Bold in 10-point on 12-point leading. Helvetica is a very useful all-round typeface. Purchase a complete Helvetica package of Black, Bold and Book, and Black Condensed, Bold Condensed and Book Condensed. The variety of weights and widths gives you great versatility. Helvetica will work for memos, graphs, display advertisements, business forms, flyers, and for headlines and captions in newsletters. Helvetica very useful all-roun

This is Helvetica Bold Italic in 10-point on 12-point leading. Helvetica is a very useful all-round typeface. Purchase a complete Helvetica package of Black, Bold and Book, and Black Condensed, Bold Condensed and Book Condensed. The variety of weights and widths gives you great versatility. Helvetica will work for memos, graphs, display advertisements, business forms, flyers, and for headlines and captions in newsletters. Helvetica is a very

Helvetica Bold Condensed in 24-point
Helvetica Bold Condensed Italic in 24-

Helvetica Bold Condensed in 18-point. Helvetica is a very useful all-purpose typeface. Purchase a complete Helvetica package of Black, Bold and Book, and Black Condensed, Bold Condensed and

This is Helvetica Condensed in 10-point on 12-point leading. Helvetica is a very useful all-round typeface. Purchase a complete Helvetica package of Black, Bold and Book, and Black Condensed, Bold Condensed and Book Condensed. The variety of weights and widths gives you great versatility. Helvetica will work for memos, graphs, display advertisements, business forms, flyers, and for headlines and captions in newsletters.This is Helvetica Condensed in ten point on twelve leading. Helvetica is a very useful all-round typeface. Purchase a complete Helvetica package of Black, Bold and Book, and

This is Helvetica Condensed Italic in 10-point on 12-point leading. Helvetica is a very useful all-round typeface. Purchase a complete Helvetica package of Black, Bold and Book, and Black Condensed, Bold Condensed and Book Condensed. The variety of weights and widths gives you great versatility. Helvetica will work for memos, graphs, display advertisements, business forms, flyers, and for headlines and captions in newsletters. This is Helvetica Condensed Italic in ten point on twelve leading.

This is Helvetica Bold Condensed in 10-point on 12-point leading. Helvetica is a very useful all-round typeface. Purchase a complete Helvetica package of Black, Bold and Book, and Black Condensed, Bold Condensed and Book Condensed. The variety of weights and widths gives you great versatility. Helvetica will work for memos, graphs, display advertisements, business forms, flyers, and for headlines and captions. This is Helvetica Bold Condensed in ten point on twelve leading. Helvetica is a very useful all-round typeface. Purchase a complete Helvetica package of Black,

This is Helvetica Condensed Bold Italic in 10-point on 12-point leading. Helvetica is a very useful all-round typeface. Purchase a complete Helvetica package of Black, Bold and Book, and Black Condensed, Bold Condensed and Book Condensed. The variety of weights and widths gives you great versatility. Helvetica will work for memos, graphs, display advertisements, business forms, flyers, and for headlines and captions in newsletters. Helvetica is a very useful all-round typeface. Purchase a

Helvetica Black in 24-point s
Helvetica Black Italic in 24-

Helvetica Black in 18-point. Helvetica is a very useful all-round typeface. Purchase a complete Helvetica package of Black, Bold and

This is Helvetica Black in 10-point on 12-point leading. Helvetica is a very useful all-round sans serif typeface. Purchase a complete Helvetica package of Black, Bold and Book, and Black Condensed, Bold Condensed and Book Condensed. The variety of weights and widths gives you great versatility. Helvetica will work for memos, captions in graphs, display advertisements,

This is Helvetica Black Italic in 10-point on 12-point leading. Helvetica is a very useful all-round sans serif typeface. Purchase a complete Helvetica package of Black, Bold and Book, and Black Condensed, Bold Condensed and Book Condensed. The variety of weights and widths gives you great versatility. Helvetica will work for memos, graphs, display advertisements, business

This is Helvetica Black Condensed in 10-point on 12-point leading. Helvetica is a very useful all-round typeface. Purchase a complete Helvetica package of Black, Bold and Book, and Black Condensed, Bold Condensed and Book Condensed. The variety of weights and widths gives you great versatility. Helvetica will work for memos, graphs, display advertisements, business forms, flyers, and for headlines and captions in newsletters. Helvetica is a very useful all-around typeface. You can use it for headlines, captions, graphs,

This is Helvetica Black Condensed Italic in 10-point on 12-point leading. Helvetica is a very useful all-round typeface. Purchase a complete Helvetica package of Black, Bold and Book, and Black Condensed, Bold Condensed and Book Condensed. The variety of weights and widths gives you great versatility. Helvetica will work for memos, graphs, display advertisements, business forms, flyers, and for headlines and captions in newsletters. Helvetica is a very useful all-around typeface. You can use it for headlines, captions, graphs,

Avant Garde Bold in 24-point siz
Avant Garde Bold Italic in 24-p

Avant Garde Bold in 18-point. Avant Garde is a modern-looking sans serif typeface. It can be used for display ads, presentations, headlines captions

This is Avant Garde in 10-point on 12-point leading. Avant Garde is a modern-looking sans serif typeface. It can be used for display ads, presentations, headlines, captions business cards, letterhead, flyers and announcements. Avant Garde is a modern-looking sans serif typeface. It can be used for display ads, presentations, headlines, captions business cards, letterhead, flyers, and announcements. This is Avant Garde in ten point on twelve

This is Avant Garde Italic in 10-point on 12-point leading. Avant Garde is a modern-looking sans serif typeface. It can be used for display ads, presentations, headlines, captions business cards, letterhead, flyers and announcements. Avant Garde is a modern-looking sans serif typeface. It can be used for display ads, presentations, headlines, captions business cards, letterhead, flyers, and announcements. This is Avant Garde in ten point on twelve

This is Avant Garde Bold in 10-point on 12-point leading. Avant Garde is a modern-looking sans serif typeface. It can be used for display ads, presentations, headlines, captions business cards, letterhead, flyers and announcements. Avant Garde is a modern-looking sans serif typeface. It can be used for display ads, presentations, headlines, captions business cards, letterhead, flyers, and announcements. This is Avant Garde in ten point on twelve

This is Avant Garde Bold Italic in 10-point on 12-point leading. Avant Garde is a modern-looking sans serif typeface. It can be used for display ads, presentations, headlines, captions business cards, letterhead, flyers and announcements. Avant Garde is a modern-looking sans serif typeface. It can be used for display ads, presentations, headlines, captions business cards, letterhead, flyers, and announcements. This is Avant Garde in

Franklin Gothic Heavy in 24-poin
Franklin Gothic Heavy Oblique i

Franklin Gothic Bold in 18-point. Franklin Gothic is a sans serif typeface with a relatively narrow set. It holds up well on frequently-copied documents such as

This is Franklin Gothic in 10-point on 12-point leading. Franklin Gothic is a sans serif typeface with a relatively narrow set. It holds up well on fre-quently-copied documents such as business forms. Use it for headlines, captions, pullout quotes, charts, and presentations. This is Franklin Gothic in ten point on twelve leading. Franklin Gothic is a sans serif typeface with a relatively narrow set. It holds up well on frequently-copied documents such as business forms. Use it for headlines,

This is Franklin Gothic Italic in 10-point on 12-point leading. Franklin Gothic is a sans serif typeface with a relatively narrow set. It holds up well on fre-quently-copied documents such as business forms. Use it for headlines, captions, pullout quotes, charts, and presentations. This is Franklin Gothic in ten point on twelve leading. Franklin Gothic is a sans serif typeface with a relatively narrow set. It holds up well on frequently-copied documents such as business forms.

This is Franklin Gothic Bold in 10-point on 12-point leading. Franklin Gothic is a sans serif typeface with a relatively narrow set. It holds up well on fre-quently-copied documents such as business forms. Use it for headlines, captions, pullout quotes, charts, and presentations. This is Franklin Gothic in ten point on twelve leading. Franklin Gothic is a sans serif typeface with a relatively narrow set. It holds up well on frequently-copied documents such as business forms. Use it for headlines,

This is Franklin Gothic Bold Italic in 10-point on 12-point leading. Franklin Gothic is a sans serif typeface with a relatively narrow set. It holds up well on frequently-copied documents such as business forms. Use it for headlines, captions, pullout quotes, charts, and presentations. This is Franklin Gothic in ten point on twelve leading. Franklin Gothic is a sans serif typeface with a relatively narrow set. It holds up well on frequently-copied documents such as business forms. Use it for headlines,

This is Brush Script in eighteen-point on thirty-point leading. Use this informal script typeface for invitations, display lines on flyers and on signs. Cursive typefaces are designed to

This is Freestyle in eighteen-point on thirty-point leading. This casual script typeface can also be used for informal invitations, signs, and for display lines on posters and flyers. Cursive typefaces are designed to emulate human handwriting or calligraphy. They are graceful and usually elegant. Some

This is Zapf Chancery in eighteen-point on thirty-point leading. This is an elegant typeface for formal invitations. Cursive typefaces are designed to emulate human handwriting or calligraphy. They are graceful

Palatino Bold in 24-point size. Pal
Palatino Bold Italic in 24-point si

Palatino Bold in 18-point. Palatino looks elegant in large headline sizes and is readable in long passages of text. You can also use it for business cards, letterhead,

This is Palatino in 10-point on 12-point leading. Palatino looks elegant in large headline sizes and is readable in long passages of text. You can also use it for business cards, letterhead, display advertisements and flyers. Palatino looks elegant in large headline sizes and is readable in long passages of text. Also use it for business cards, letterhead, display advertisements and flyers. Palatino looks elegant in large headline sizes and is readable in long passages of text. Also use it for business cards, letterhead, dis

This is Palatino Italic in 10-point on 12-point leading. Palatino looks elegant in large headline sizes and is readable in long passages of text. You can also use it for business cards, letterhead, display advertisements and flyers. Palatino looks elegant in large headline sizes and is readable in long passages of text. Also use it for business cards, letterhead, display advertisements and flyers. Palatino looks elegant in large headline sizes and is readable in long passages of text. Also use it for business cards, letterhead, display advertisements and flyers.

This is Palatino Bold in 10-point on 12-point leading. Palatino looks elegant in large headline sizes and is readable in long passages of text. You can also use it for business cards, letterhead, display advertisements and flyers. Palatino looks elegant in large headline sizes and is readable in long passages of text. Also use it for business cards, letterhead, display advertisements and flyers. Palatino looks elegant in large headline sizes and is readable in long passages of text. Also use it

This is Palatino Bold Italic in 10-point on 12-point leading. Palatino looks elegant in large headline sizes and is readable in long passages of text. You can also use it for business cards, letterhead, display advertisements and flyers. Palatino looks elegant in large headline sizes and is readable in long passages of text. Also use it for business cards, letterhead, display advertisements and flyers. Palatino looks elegant in large headline sizes and is readable in long passages of text. Also use it for business

Souvenir Bold in 24-point size.
Souvenir Bold Italic in 24-poi

Souvenir Bold in 18-point. Souvenir is an informal typeface with rounded serifs. It's interesting in display size and readable in text size, you can also use if

This is Souvenir in 10-point on 12-point leading. Souvenir is an informal typeface with rounded serifs. It's interesting in display size and readable in text size, you can also use it for presentations, flyers and display advertisements. Souvenir is an informal typeface with rounded serifs. It's interesting in display size and readable in text size, you can also use it for presentations, flyers and display advertisements. Souvenir is an informal typeface with rounded serifs. It's interesting in display size and readable in text size, you can also

This is Souvenir Italic in 10-point on 12-point leading. Souvenir is an informal typeface with rounded serifs. It's interesting in display size and readable in text size, you can also use it for presentations, flyers and display advertisements. Souvenir is an informal typeface with rounded serifs. It's interesting in display size and readable in text size, you can also use it for presentations, flyers and display advertisements. Souvenir is an informal typeface with rounded serifs. It's interesting in displa

This is Souvenir Bold in 10-point on 12-point leading. Souvenir is an informal typeface with rounded serifs. It's interesting in display size and readable in text size, you can also use it for presentations, flyers and display advertisements. Souvenir is an informal typeface with rounded serifs. It's interesting in display size and readable in text size, you can also use it for presentations, flyers and display advertisements. Souvenir is an informal typeface with rou

This is Souvenir Bold Italic in 10-point on 12-point leading. Souvenir is an informal typeface with rounded serifs. It's interesting in display size and readable in text size, you can also use it for presentations, flyers and display advertisements. Souvenir is an informal typeface with rounded serifs. It's interesting in display size and readable in text size, you can also use it for presentations, flyers and display advertisements.

Optima Bold in 24-point size. Opti
Optima Bold Italic in 24-point size.

Optima Bold in 18-point. Optima is another very handy contemporary typeface. Though at first glance it looks like a sans serif typeface, on closer inspection it has very slight serifs.

This is Optima in 10-point on 12-point leading. Optima is another very handy contemporary typeface. Though at first glance it looks like a sans serif typeface, on closer inspection it has very slight serifs. It's especially useful for those times when you need a practical typeface that holds up well on often-copied documents. Optima has a relatively narrow set. Optima is another very handy contemporary typeface. Though at first glance it looks like a sans serif typeface, on closer inspection it has very slight ser

This is Optima Italic in 10-point on 12-point leading. Optima is another very handy contemporary typeface. Though at first glance it looks like a sans serif typeface, on closer inspection it has very slight serifs. It's especially useful for those times when you need a practical typeface that holds up well on often-copied documents. Optima has a relatively narrow set. Optima is another very handy contemporary typeface. Though at first glance it looks like a sans serif typeface, on closer inspection it has very slight ser

This is Optima Bold in 10-point on 12-point leading. Optima is another very handy contemporary typeface. Though at first glance it looks like a sans serif typeface, on closer inspection it has very slight serifs. It's especially useful for those times when you need a practical typeface that holds up well on often-copied documents. Optima has a relatively narrow set. Optima is another very handy contemporary typeface. Though at first glance it looks like a sans serif typeface, on closer inspection it has very

This is Optima Bold Italic in 10-point on 12-point leading. Optima is another very handy contemporary typeface. Though at first glance it looks like a sans serif typeface, on closer inspection it has very slight serifs. It's especially useful for those times when you need a practical typeface that holds up well on often-copied documents. Optima has a relatively narrow set. Optima is another very handy contemporary typeface. Though at first glance it looks like a sans serif typeface, on closer inspection it has very

Lubalin Graph Bold in 24-point
Lubalin Graph Bold Italic in 24

Lubalin Graph Bold in 18-point. Lubalin Graph is a square serif typeface, also known as slab serif. It is a good typeface to use for headlines, cutlines extensive

This is Lubalin Graph in 10-point on 12-point leading. Lubalin Graph is a square serif typeface, also known as slab serif. This serif design doesn't work too well for extensive amounts of text, but is good for headlines and captions of less formal documents. Also use it for flyers, announcements, and display advertisements. Lubalin Graph is a square serif typeface, also known as slab serif. This serif design doesn't work too well for extensive text, but is good for head

This is Lubalin Graph Italic in 10-point on 12-point leading. Lubalin Graph is a square serif typeface, also known as slab serif. This serif design doesn't work too well for extensive amounts of text, but is good for headlines and captions of less formal documents. Also use it for flyers, announcements, and display advertisements. Lubalin Graph is a square serif typeface, also known as slab serif. This serif design doesn't work too well for extensive text, but is

This is Lubalin Graph Bold in 10-point on 12-point leading. Lubalin Graph is a square serif typeface, also known as slab serif. This serif design doesn't work too well for extensive amounts of text, but is good for headlines and captions of less formal documents. Also use it for flyers, announcements, and display advertisements. Lubalin Graph is a square serif typeface, also known as slab serif. This serif design doesn't work too well for extensive text, but

This is Lubalin Graph Bold Italic in 10-point on 12-point leading. Lubalin Graph is a square serif typeface, also known as slab serif. This serif design doesn't work too well for extensive amounts of text, but is good for headlines and captions of less formal documents. Also use it for flyers, announcements, and display advertisements. Lubalin Graph is a square serif typeface, also known as slab serif. This serif design doesn't work too well for extensive t

CHAPTER

Typing to Typesetting

Once you've created text in a word processing program it needs some changes, or clean-up, before you place it into a page makeup program. At this point, you're finished as a writer-typist and begin functioning as a typesetter. Typesetting is an undervalued profession, as you're soon to find out, but much of the tedium and attention to detail can be taken out of it by letting the computer do the routine tasks. This chapter will show you what to instruct your computer to do and why. It should also enable you to judge when computer-generated solutions are inappropriate.

Changes to your word processor text are necessary because the routine methods of expression that are adequate when banging out a document on a typewriter look especially inelegant when typeset. The goal of typesetting is to pave a smooth road on which the reader's eyes can cruise at full speed, unhindered. Typewriter conventions, such as using two hyphens instead of a long dash, or using foot and inch marks instead of apostrophes, act as potholes in that road. They jar the reader's concentration away from the message.

The public reads professionally-typeset publications daily, in which much attention is paid to details. If your document is obviously desktop and somewhat difficult to read, it is at an immediate disadvantage.

What to Change

1. *Use only one wordspace between sentences.*

Typist are trained to use two wordspaces between sentences. This style does not apply to typesetting because it creates unsightly white gaps or streaks that appear to be rivers of white within text blocks. Use your word processor's search and replace tool to remove the extra wordspace between sentences.

2. *Use an em dash wherever you would use double hyphens on a typewritten document.*

When setting text-size type, use an em dash (a dash the width of the point size of type) where you would use double hyphens on a typewriter. Example: "DOS--Disk Operating System--is a toothache to learn." Substitute one em dash for each set of double hyphens in that sentence. An em dash looks like this: — (see Figure 23).

When setting larger than text-size type however, it's better to substitute an en dash (a dash the width of 50 percent of the type's point size) for the double hyphens, because a full em dash looks too long in large sizes. Also use an en dash, rather than a hyphen, when denoting "from . . . to" as in dates. Example: January 23–25. An en dash looks like this: – (see Figure 23).

3. *Don't use inch marks instead of double quotes and don't use foot marks instead of single quotes or apostrophes.*

Inch marks (") and foot marks (') are not the same as quotes (" " ') or apostrophes and closing single quotes (') even if desktop publishing documentation euphemistically calls them "neutral quotes."

Inch marks and foot marks should only be used

Don't use two word spaces between sentences. That's for typewriters only. In typesetting, it creates unsightly white gaps in text. These streaks appear to be rivers of white within text blocks. Use your word processor's search and replace tool to remove those extra word spaces between sentences.

This—is an em dash.
This--should be changed to an em dash.

An en dash (–) should be used in 'from . . . to' situations such as dates: June 10–October 21

'Impressive?'
'Impressive.'

Figure 23.

as symbols to convey measurements. Using them as quotes and apostrophes in typeset material looks crude and can confuse readers. Always use the true typeset quotes and apostrophes for everything other than inch and foot measurements.

Conversion Routine

When importing word processor-created documents, many page makeup programs automatically convert inch marks to typeset double quotes, foot marks to opening single quotes and closing single quotes, and change foot marks within words to apostrophes. They will also convert double hyphens to em dashes.

One catch though, these conversion programs aren't smart enough to distinguish where an apostrophe (') rather than an opening single quote (') is necessary. (Remember that apostrophes—which look exactly the same as closing single quotes—are used whenever something is missing from a word, such as *it's* as a contraction for *it is,* or when using the possessive form of a noun, as *Jean's computer.* Figures, letters, signs and abbreviations form their plurals by adding apostrophe *s,* such as *6's, VIP's.*)

With conversion programs, the problem is that whenever a single neutral quote, (foot mark) is found *after* a wordspace and immediately before a word or number, an opening single quote (') is substituted because the program assumes it to be the start of a quoted section. You get *'seventies* or *'70's* (short for nineteen-seventies) instead of the proper 'seventies or '70's.

Word Divisions

Back when printers set type line by line, we concentrated much attention on where to divide and hyphenate a word at the end of a line on which it would not entirely fit. The general idea was to divide a word on a syllable, but also to divide it in the way that the word is pronounced. Therefore, not all syllables were considered appropriate places to divide words. For instance, *connection* should be divided between the two consonants that are pronounced separately—connec-tion—not con-nection, where the two consonants are pronounced together.

Computers can be given limited hyphenation dictionaries and algorithmic word division formulas, but they surely don't know pronunciation from pro-creation. When computers started to handle word divisions in typesetting composition in the '60's and '70's, word division standards went into a steep decline. The original typesetting computers came up with some entertaining word divisions, such as *association* divided ass-ociation.

Over the past 20 years of reading computer-generated word divisions in books, newspapers and magazines, readers have gotten used to what printers call bad word breaks. This means that as readers, we're often fooled into thinking that we're going to read say, *proj*ect (task) when *proj*ect (to plan) is divided proj- and -ect is run over to the next line. Another example is *present*. *Pre*sent, meaning to give, should be divided pre-sent as it is pronounced. *Pre*sent, meaning a gift (also meaning now-existing), should be divided pres-ent.

Computer systems are getting better at word division problems though. When you think about it, it's amazing that a microcomputer has enough memory and programming elegance to use a hyphenation and exception dictionary, and with many systems, you only wait a half-second for it to complete this complex task.

Here are a few other things that you should watch for on word divisions:

Try to break no more than two words in a row in text blocks. Three hyphenated line endings in a row make it easy for the reader to accidentally jump over the second consecutively hyphenated line.

Don't divide words of fewer than six letters.

Avoid carrying over two-letter syllables. An example is adaptabili-ty.

Single letter syllables should never stand alone: Example: a-lone.

Figure 24. The dollar sign is used only on the first line of tables and before totals. Figures with decimals align on the decimals. Columns of whole numbers and fractions align on the last whole number. Roman numerals align on the right. Words align on the left.

Points of alignment.

$	90.50	32.01	1 ¼	I.	Revenues
	80.45	.001	3	II.	Expenses
	(6.00)	100.5	14 ½	III.	Earnings
	100.00	4.5	2 ¾	IV.	Extra Items
$	270.95	137.011	21 ½	V.	Totals

Tables of Numbers

There are some kinds of information which, when set in tabular form, are more easily read and digested and more forcefully presented than when set in straight paragraph form. Examples are newspaper stock market listings and columns of figures in a business plan. Here is how to set tabular information in a way that's thoughtful of your readers.

Generally, all words are aligned to the left and figures are aligned to the right. Figures containing decimals should align on their decimals. Columns of whole numbers with fractions line up on the last whole number. In columns of figures representing dollars, the dollar sign is used only at the top of the column and before totals. Roman numerals align on the right (see Figure 24).

Avoid breaking tables up onto more than one page. If it's necessary, repeat the column headers and title from the previous page. Put a *(continued)* after the title (see Figure 25).

Figure 25.

PAGE 11

YEAR'S PERFORMANCE IN REVIEW

Name	Close	Change	Fri.	Last
International Paper	$56.60	+9.24	57.40	59.06
Texaco	58.88	+8.78	53.02	58.11
Procter & Gamble	33.80	-5.24	32.38	33.46
Bethlehem Steel	64.88	+3.78	54.73	52.60
McDonald's	86.60	+9.84	75.26	47.95
United Technology	39.58	-8.76	40.54	43.90
Alcoa	36.60	-9.14	42.45	27.06
3M	53.88	+8.78	53.02	38.32
Coca-Cola	40.89	+8.25	55.12	33.60
General Electric	38.60	-9.22	36.32	36.06
Apple Computers	55.87	+8.73	40.02	

PAGE 12

YEAR'S PERFORMANCE IN REVIEW (Continued)

Name	Close	Change	Fri.	Last
Westinghouse	$56.60	+9.24	57.40	59.06
Boeing	58.88	+8.78	53.02	58.11
Chevron	33.80	-5.24	32.38	33.46
Sears Roebuck	64.88	+3.78	54.73	52.60
Merck	86.60	+9.84	75.26	47.95
American Express	39.58	-8.76	40.54	43.90
Philip Morris	36.60	-9.14	42.45	27.06
Primerica	53.88	+8.78	53.02	38.32
Navistar	40.89	+8.25	55.12	33.60
Allied-Signal	38.60	-9.22	36.32	36.06
Goodyear	55.87	+8.73	40.02	

Difficult to follow:

Player	**Avg.**
Guy Dean	.500
Jean Susan	.485
Bernard Lewis	.400
Donna Jean White-Smith	.375

Much better:

Player	**Avg.**	**Player**	**Avg.**
Guy Dean	.500	Bernard Lewis	.400
Jean Susan	.485	Donna Jean White-Smith	.375

Word space · Leaders · En space · Em space · Hanging indention

Figure 26. Dividing a wide column into two columns makes comprehension of information easier and saves space. Repeat header at top of each column. Separate numbers from leaders with an en space. This makes the numbers stand out clearly.

Leaders (most commonly a string of periods) are an excellent way of leading the eye from one point to another in a table (see Figure 26). Begin leaders within a wordspace (three-em space) of the words that they follow and end them about an en space or more from the numbers that end the line. This allows the numbers to stand out clearly and it keeps the leaders away from any decimal points that may begin a number. The leaders must all line up evenly on the right.

Nothing will make just a few words or figures on a very wide table look good though, including leaders. When faced with this problem, make two columns and repeat the column headers on each one.

If a line has too many words to fit in its column space, break it into two lines in a hanging indention. A *hanging indention* is one where the first line is set to the full measure and subsequent lines are all indented on the left by a uniform amount, commonly an em space (see Figure 26, bottom right).

Ditto marks in tabular matter are not considered proper for anything other than words; don't use them on numbers. Also, they are only used if a word is repeated at least three times in a row. Parenthetical figures should be used only to state negative numbers, not to separate a numbered item from the rest of the line, outline style.

Quotes in Text

If a quote in text goes longer than three lines, you should make a separate paragraph. It should be set in type one point size smaller than the text, indented on both sides, and separated above and below with extra paragraph space to make it stand out.

On wide columns the indention for quotes can be as wide as one-half inch each side. On narrow columns the indention can be as small as one em on either side, as in the following example:

> "In successively running quoted paragraphs, quotation marks are used at the beginning but not the end of each paragraph, until the last paragraph.
>
> It's also acceptable, if the quotation is indented, to leave the quotation marks off entirely."

In the United States, a quote within a quote is denoted with single quote marks: "Greg mentioned Clark's comment, 'I hate DOS,' at the meeting." To denote another quote within the single quote—if Greg quoted Clark quoting a third person—it should be bracketed with double quote marks. By alternating between double and single quote marks, you can denote as many quotes within quotes as necessary.

To separate a single quote from a double quote, put the punctuation between them, as in this sentence: "Greg said Nancy told him, 'Small text should be set in shadowed, outline type, all capitals'." If there's no punctuation to separate the single and double quotes, use a thin space. Otherwise, punctuation should always go *before* the closing quote unless you need it to separate single from double quotes.

By the way, that advice of Nancy's is not helpful.

Rhyming Poetry

If you have occasion to set poetry that actually rhymes (it's not *that* unusual), here are the traditional typesetting guidelines.

Rhyming poetry is set flush left. Lines that rhyme with each other within the same stanza should line up with each other on the left. If they are indented on the left, they should each be indented by the same amount, like these lines by Robert Service:

> *The Northern Lights have seen queer sights,*
>   *But the queerest they ever did see*
> *Was that night on the marge of Lake Lebarge*
>   *I cremated Sam McGee.*
>
> *Now Sam McGee was from Tennessee . . .*

Don't make the mistake of centering the poem horizontally on the page on the longest line. Centering it on the *average* line length will give the page a much more balanced look.

Lines of the poem that go too long to fit on one line should be indented one em space more than any other indented line in the poem.

Ligatures

Figure 27.

Because of the shape of the lowercase *f,* its projecting top stroke ends up on top of the upper part of the *l* and on top of the dot over the *i* when it's set immediately before either one without letterspacing. The ligatures fl and fi were created to solve this problem (see Figure 27).

If you have a practical way of putting ligatures in, such as a search and replace function, it's a refined touch to substitute ligatures for fl and fi combinations, especially in large type. Most desktop hyphenation programs and spell-checkers will not recognize words containing ligatures though, that is a problem. Another consideration is that on any justified lines with letterspacing—where you don't need and should not use ligatures—you'll have to go back and take them out.

Scout around to find where the ligatures are located on your keyboard map. Once you find their location, write it down since you'll probably not use them too often.

In Summary

Typing rules don't apply to typesetting. By using typesetting conventions, your document will be more elegant to look at and easier to read.

- Don't use inch or foot marks instead of true quotation marks and apostrophes.
- Use an em dash rather than double hyphens.
- Never put more than one wordspace between sentences.
- Double check the word divisions that your program creates for you.
- Quotes in text that go longer than three lines should be set one size smaller in a separate paragraph and indented on either side.
- Quotes within quotes are denoted with single quote marks.

CHAPTER 6

Graphic Design

Graphic design is not art, and it's not decoration added on to a publication, like those tailfins on old Cadillacs. Further, creating and producing an interesting newsletter, a distinctive business card, or an easy-to-follow training manual doesn't require inspiration. Think of graphic design as presentation. Good designs simply remove obstacles between the reader and the information; they present a message in an inviting and easily-read format.

A poor design will attempt to dress things up, becoming a distracting obstacle to communication. Effective designs get out of the readers' way and subordinate all artistic impulses to the readers' comfort and comprehension.

First, give readers optimum wordspacing in your type and set it in lowercase as much as possible. Choose a suitable typeface family for your purpose and use it in moderate line lengths. Clean up your word processor documents using typesetting conventions. Then, create straightforward designs.

Desktop publishing software can deliver novel and elaborate design attributes but the most important rule of successful document design is *keep it simple*. Simple designs communicate effectively and have a pleasing appearance. Most messages beg for straightforward design treatment. Use type, rules and illustrations in their infinite combinations. Only use borders, screens, ornaments and clip art sparingly. If a design element doesn't have some vital thing to contribute to the subject, then don't even consider using it.

You can buy many books that deal with the subject of publication design from an art perspective: ones that explore Futurism, Dada, Art Deco, and the creative concept. But first, learn such practical things as where to position type on a title page, and how to determine appropriate page margins.

It's most helpful to look for a clean, attractively-designed document with a purpose similar to your project. Measure its page size, count the columns, find a comparable typeface. Use these things as a point of departure for your own design.

Rather than set your sights on an artistic masterpiece, establish useful, attainable goals for the design of your publication. Your objective might well be to create a document that's inviting to look at, easily-read and delivered on time.

Design of Text

The design generally should begin with the text, and a choice of typeface for it that's fitting to what's being communicated. When selecting among roman styles for text type—and you should use roman type for large amounts of text—remember that it's important to select a light to medium weight face. Text in a typeface that is too light cannot be easily distinguished from its background, and pages of dark, heavy text are uninviting to readers. New Century Schoolbook is an example of a medium weight text typeface. New Baskerville and Garamond are examples of light weight text faces (see pages 45-47).

For text purposes, rule out modern roman typefaces that have a high contrast between their thick and thin strokes, such as Bodoni. The extremely thin strokes are difficult to distinguish in text sizes and the thick strokes reduce the visibility of the counter-forms—those enclosed white spaces in a letter. Such characteristics give a page of text an intimidating dazzle.

Roman oldstyle typefaces are especially good for

text because they generally have a small x-height and so have extra white space naturally designed-in between lines. This means they require less leading and are more inviting to read in long passages.

Typefaces that have short ascenders and descenders, and have lowercase letters with large x-heights—such as New Century Schoolbook and Souvenir—are greatly improved by extra leading when used for text.

Justified or Ragged?

In order to read text comfortably, one must be able to find the beginning of each consecutive line quickly and easily over and over again. This is not a problem when type is set so that the left edge of each typeset line is aligned with the left margin. If the copy is centered, or is aligned on the right only, the reader has to search to find the beginning of each line. Therefore, there are only two prudent choices of line arrangements when setting full pages or long columns of type: Justified, or aligned left with ragged right (see Figure 28).

If your columns are narrow, justified type can be difficult to read because the lines often become noticeably letterspaced and have excessive wordspacing leaving rivers of white space within the text (see Figure 7, page 18), and making some paragraphs look darker than others. When using narrow column widths, it's better to set your columns aligned on the left and ragged right. This way the wordspacing is even and no letterspacing is inserted, and you will get a uniform typographic color in each paragraph.

When your text's column measure is comfortably wide (see Figure 6, page 17), you can choose between flush left/ragged right and justified copy. Generally justified text looks formal, and flush left text has a casual look.

In **justified** copy, the type is aligned on both the left and right margins by varying the amount of spacing between words — and sometimes between letters — in each line. It has a formal look.

This is copy set **flush left** and ragged right. The lines have exactly the same amount of wordspacing. No letterspacing is used. The left-aligned margin makes it easy to find the beginning of each line.

This is **flush right** and ragged left copy. It has equal wordspacing and no letterspacing. When used in long passages though, it's tiresome for the reader to find the beginning of each line.

This is **centered** copy. It's ragged on both the left and right sides. It's not suitable for text.

Figure 28.

Maintain Text Style

Decide on the typeface, point size and leading for your publication's text and adhere to it throughout the document. Using more than one point size of type or more than one typeface family for text within a publication contributes to a busy look which is uninviting to readers.

The problem with varying text's leading within a page or between pages and columns is that it destroys text's even typographic color. Paragraphs with less leading look darker than the rest (see Figure 29). This irregularity also contributes to a busy look and gives pages a poorly planned appearance.

Figure 29. Varying text's leading within a document causes the columns and paragraphs with less leading to look darker than the rest. Also, when spacing paragraphs, add slightly less space after paragraphs with a short last line and slightly more space after ones with a full last line, in order to make them appear equally spaced.

Varying text's leading within a page or between pages and columns destroys its even typographic color. Paragraphs with less leading look darker than the rest. This irregularity gives pages a poorly planned and busy appearance.

Paragraph with 11-point leading.

Maintain a consistent text style throughout a publication. Add space in moderate amounts *between* paragraphs to fill out pages and columns.

Paragraph with 10-point leading.

Within a column or a page the space between each paragraph should appear to be equal.

Add slightly less space after a paragraph with a short last line, because it has some built-in white space, and slightly more space after a paragraph with a full last line, in order to make them appear to have an equal amount of space between them.

6 points of extra space between paragraphs.

The maximum amount of extra space between paragraphs should be about 3/5ths of the amount of your text's leading.

4 points of extra space between paragraphs.

For these reasons, if your page makeup program has a feature called Vertical Justification, don't use it to vary your text's leading. Only use it to adjust the space *between* paragraphs in text (see Paragraph Spacing, next section).

When deliberating on the amount of leading for your text, remember that adding space between lines of text results in greatly increased readability. If you want your page to be inviting and easy to read, don't be stingy with the leading. Edit out some of the copy instead of reducing your text's leading from its optimum amount. Adding too much leading in text will first show between paragraphs where the white space on the last line of one paragraph meets the beginning indention of the next. But extra text leading will seldom seem excessive to your readers.

Paragraph Spacing

Maintaining a consistent text style throughout a publication does not mean that you have no control over how long your text goes, or how it is divided among columns or pages. Adding space in moderate amounts *between* paragraphs helps fill out pages and columns. It also gives readers some breathing room. If you're using a text style that doesn't have paragraph indentions, space between paragraphs is essential to indicate when a new paragraph begins.

Within a column or a page, it's best if the space between each paragraph appears to be equal. This means spacing visually rather than mechanically. Add slightly less space after a paragraph with a short last line, because it has some built-in white space, and slightly more space after a paragraph with a full last line, in order to make them appear equally spaced (see Figure 29).

The maximum amount of extra space between paragraphs should be about 3/5ths of your text's leading. In text with 12-point leading for example, the maximum amount of extra space between paragraphs should be about 7 or 8 points. Adding more than this will make paragraphs, of narrow columns at least, appear to be unrelated.

Generally, an informal document such as a newsletter can have a greater amount space between paragraphs without looking sloppy, than can a more formal document, such as a business plan.

Using Subheads

Subheads are minor headlines within text. They should be the same point size and family of type as the text and set in boldface. Subheads may be part of the outline of the material and introduce subjects or they may only be different phrases taken from the text they will appear near, like the subhead immediately below.

'Somewhat Grey'

There are several advantages to using subheads in long passages of text. Newspaper people who use subheads often, say that they are to "keep the reader's eyes rested and interested." Columns composed entirely of text can appear somewhat grey and monotonous. Adding boldface subheads to long passages of text gives it enough contrast to make it more inviting to read, less tiring on the eyes, and easier for your readers to find their place if they've been distracted away. Using subheads maintains the needed regularity of the style of text, where too much contrast would be distracting and therefore counterproductive.

Using subheads throughout your text will also give you flexibility in its length. If you have one text line too many at the bottom of a page, you can gain the space by removing a subhead. If your text is one line short in a column, you can write and insert a subhead.

Spacing Heads

A common mistake is to think that space should be equalized above and below a headline or subhead. This is not so. A headline goes with the text that follows it. You should organize, or cluster the headline with its text, making the relationship obvious to the reader. The important thing to remember about all headlines, including subheads, is that you should always put more space *above* them than below them.

A good proportion for dividing space above and below heads is two to one. For every extra point of space you put below a headline, make sure you insert at least two points of space above it.

Figure 30.

A widow in text happens when the last typeset line of a paragraph is carried over on its own to the next column or page. This leaves a short line alone at the top of the column or page. The natural white space at the end of this short line of type blends in with the upper page margin's white space. ——————— Widow

An orphan is a short word, or a short part of a word, that's left over at the end of a paragraph and comprises the entire last line. It's not necessarily left alone at the top of a page or column as a widow is. ——————— Orphan

It's always best to bring down a word from

Widows in Text

A widow in text is when the last typeset line of a paragraph is carried over on its own to the next column or page. This leaves a short line alone at the top of a column or page. The natural white space at the end of that short line of type blends in with the surrounding white space of the upper margin and leaves an unsightly white gap where the definite, dark image edge of a typeset line is needed (see Figure 30).

Definitions of a widow vary though. Some publishers insist on carrying over at least the two last lines of a paragraph to avoid a widow. Others consider that a full line (one that has enough words to fill out the entire line), even if it's the last line of a paragraph, cannot be a widow.

Either way that you define it, a widow is a bad break. Now, in typography, a bad break is not something to be shrugged off philosophically as *karma,* or fate, it implies that some action is required to resolve the problem. In this case, you should redistribute your lines of type over its columns or pages, respacing in order to give the widow its preceding line as a companion. This will either be back with the rest of the paragraph or onto the next page or column with at least one other line from the same paragraph.

To solve a widow problem, you can vary the space above and below subheads or add a few points of extra space between paragraphs. Your design may even allow you to leave an unequal amount of lines of text in columns or pages. But for a neat, pleasingly-shaped page of type, don't leave widows. Also, be careful not to create a new widow somewhere else when re-running your text over columns and pages.

Orphans in Text

An orphan is a short word—or short part of a word—that's left over at the end of a paragraph and comprises the entire last line. It's not necessarily left alone at the *top* of a page or a column, like a widow.

In typesetting, orphan-hood is a less serious transgression than widow-hood. Widows leave too much white space at the top of columns or type pages where it is undesired, orphans leave white space within the text page, which is much more acceptable, but still can be unsightly (see Figure 30).

As is the case with widows, standards vary on the minimum appropriate amount of letters in a word or part of a word to leave as the last line of a paragraph. A reasonable guideline is to call anything under five characters, left alone as the last line of a paragraph, an orphan. Watch for orphans and bring another word down to the last line to give it a companion.

Initial Letters

AN INITIAL LETTER, also know as a drop cap, is the oversize capital letter at the beginning of a paragraph, such as the *A* at the beginning of this one. It may be larger or smaller, the design possibilities are far-reaching. Initial letters are often used at the beginning of chapters or the start of sections in books.

Most typesetters and desktop publishers don't know how to, or don't take the time to follow through on important aspects of initial letter design. Therefore, this is a good opportunity to make your own text pages uncommonly attractive and easy to read.

In the early days of moveable type, the alphabet had only capital letters. When lowercase letters were invented for increased readability, printers quit using all capitals for the body of text. Capitals are harder to read but they can briefly command attention, so printers kept using all capitals at the start of a section or chapter to draw readers' attention to the appropriate place to begin.

From this, the initial letter arrangement developed. The first letter of the first word is a capital letter of exaggerated size, the first few words are set in text-sized capitals or small caps, and the following lowercase text is indented on the left side to accommodate the large initial letter.

The size of the large initial letter and the extra white space around it stop a reader's page scan and leave no doubt as to where to begin reading. The three sizes of the type involved: a large capital letter, a few words in caps, then the lowercase letters, go from left to right and from large to small, funneling reader's attention and drawing them into the text. It's an effective design technique.

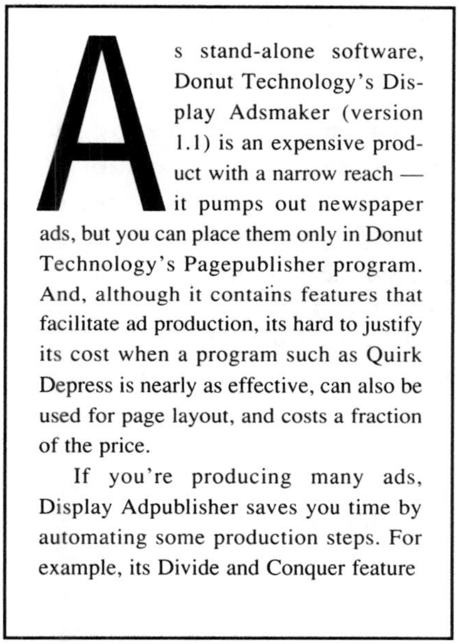

A
s stand-alone software, Donut Technology's Display Adsmaker (version 1.1) is an expensive product with a narrow reach — it pumps out newspaper ads, but you can place them only in Donut Technology's Pagepublisher program. And, although it contains features that facilitate ad production, its hard to justify its cost when a program such as Quirk Depress is nearly as effective, can also be used for page layout, and costs a fraction of the price.

If you're producing many ads, Display Adpublisher saves you time by automating some production steps. For example, its Divide and Conquer feature

Figure 31. This is typical of the poorly-crafted drop caps seen today.

Often today drop caps are put together by an arbitrary mechanically-spaced formula that ignores individual capital letter shapes and so is unnecessarily difficult to read. This problem is easily seen in the example on the left (see Figure 31).

Here's how to design your drop caps in a manner that's thoughtful to the way your audience reads.

Always butt up the first line of type closely against the initial letter. Otherwise the reader has to make note of the initial letter, then search for the rest of the word that goes with it. Parts of words are particularly difficult to find because people read by recognizing whole words at a glance, they aren't used to putting pieces of words together. One of the primary reasons for using an initial letter is to funnel the readers' eyes fluidly into the text at the start of a section, so an interruption, causing readers to search for the rest of a word begun by an initial letter, is counterproductive.

On initial letters that are vertical on the right side, such as the *H* or *M,* the first line of text should butt up against the initial letter and subsequent lines should be indented by an en space—fifty percent of the text type size—away from it (see Figure 32). If these lines are not indented more deeply than the first text line, the reader must make note of the initial letter then find the rest of the word with which it belongs among identically indented lines. For easy reading, it's much better to have the remainder of the first word, which is begun by the large initial letter, obviously closer to that initial letter than any other word or part of a word.

If the initial letter slants back to the left, from top to bottom on its right-hand side, such as a *F, P, V, W* or *Y,* no additional indention is necessary because it would add an unsightly gap to the white space created by the contour of the letter itself. The same is true of the *A* and *L* and of most italic initial letters.

Hᴇʀᴇ ɪꜱ ᴛʜᴇ ᴡᴀʏ to arrange the text around an initial letter that is vertical on the right side, like the H or M. The first line of text should butt up against the initial letter and subsequent lines should be indented by approximately an en space away from it.

Wʜᴇɴ ᴀɴ ɪɴɪᴛɪᴀʟ letter slants back to the left like an F, P, V, W or Y, no additional indention is necessary because it would add an unsightly gap to the white space created by the contour of the letter itself. The same is true of the A and L and also most italic initial letters.

"Tʜᴇ ᴛᴏᴘ ᴏꜰ an initial letter should always be at or above the top of the first line of text. Its baseline should line up evenly with the baseline of the last indented line of text type, otherwise the letter will appear to be hanging alone, without a definite relationship to the text.

Figure 32.

After the large initial letter, set the first few words of the paragraph in either all caps or small caps. This acts as a transition—the middle part of the funnel—from the large initial letter down to the lowercase text of the paragraph.

In our culture we read from top to bottom and

from left to right, so the top of an initial letter should always be at or above the top of the first line of text. This ensures that the reader will see the initial letter first, then the remainder of the first word. The bottom of an initial letter should always line up evenly with the bottom of the baseline of the last indented line of text type. In this way the initial letter does not appear to be hanging alone in space, but has a definite relationship to the text.

Opening quotes that go before an initial letter should be set in a size closer to the size of the text than the size of the initial letter. Positioning the quotes in the left margin looks best (see Figure 32, bottom).

Text Depth

Sometimes it's helpful to determine what point size your text will be before you bring it into your page makeup program. If your word processor gives you a character count, you can easily figure out the approximate length of your text in any point size, column width and leading.

The basis of this copy-fitting formula is that the average English word consists of five letters. Each word requires a wordspace, so the average English word uses a total of six characters. The width of six characters on a line is equivalent to about three ems of type, depending upon the set of the typeface. (Remember that an em is the width of the size of type being used—10-point type has ems 10 points wide.)

If you absolutely hate story problems, skip this section and go on to the next chapter. Come back later if you find the formula may be helpful to you.

If you know that your columns will be 15 picas wide, you can calculate approximately how many lines your copy will make in 10-point type. First figure out how many ems of 10-point type are in a line 15 picas wide. To do this, convert the pica measure to points. 15 picas multiplied by 12, which is the amount of points per pica, equals 180 points. So, a 15-pica line is 180 points across.

An em of 10-point type is 10 points wide, so di-

If your columns are 15 picas wide, how many lines of type will your copy make in ten point?

15 x 12 [points per pica]   =180 [column width in points]

Then:

180 ÷ 10 [width of 10-point em =18 [amount of ems of 10-point in
          in points]   15 pica column]

18 ems of 10-point type will fit on each 15 pica line. Each word is approximately three ems wide, so:

   18 [ems of 10-point per line]

÷ 3 [ems per word]

= 6 [amount of words in 10-point type that will fit on each line]

Your character count divided by 6—the average number of characters per word—is the number of words in your copy.

If you use 10-point type with 12-point leading you must add in the extra two points per line to get the actual depth of your copy.

Figure 33.

vide 180 points by 10 points. The answer is 18. That means you can get 18 ems of 10-point type on each line 15 picas wide. Since each word takes about 3 ems and each line is 18 ems wide, divide 18 ems by 3 ems. The answer, six, means that six words will fit on each line.

From here you divide the total number of words in your copy by 6, because you've established that 6 words will fit on each 15-pica line. That answer will give you the approximate number of lines your copy will make in 10-point type (see Figure 33). If you set your 10-point type on 12-point leading, you must add in the extra two points for each line to give you the actual depth your copy will make.

If your copy goes too long, try the same formula substituting 9-point type. An em of 9-point type is 9 points wide. There are 180 points across the line as established above, and 180 divided by 9 is 20. So, 20 ems of 9-point type will fit on every line. Each word taking about 3 ems, divide 20 by 3 and the result is

6.5 words per line. Divide the total amount of words in your copy by 6.5 to get the total amount of lines your text will make in 9-point type. Don't forget to add in the extra leading between lines to arrive at its total depth.

In Summary

- Always design simply. Eliminate any non-essential graphic elements.
- Maintain a consistent text style throughout your publication.
- Be generous with text leading.
- Always put more space above headlines than below them.

Page Design

A desktop publishing system, like any computer system, measures objects with extreme precision. It will accurately center type on pages to within a fraction of a point. While this makes it an excellent publishing tool, it's only half the solution to design problems. Human visual perception is not mechanical, for example, a page of text with equal margins on the top and bottom make the block of text appear to be positioned low on the paper. The ability to measure space precisely on a page is important, but learning to apportion that space in a way that's pleasing to the eccentricities of human perception is the other half of the procedure.

Proportions—the ratio of height to width—is another vital aspect of good design. Some proportions are pleasing, others are not. For example, an exact square is viewed as unattractive, you seldom see publications designed in that shape.

Appropriate page proportions, the shape of artwork, and apportioning margin space are not obvious, intuitive or logical choices. Traditional graphic design guidelines work well here, and can save you hours of experimentation in your efforts to create professional-looking pages.

Optical Center

The following is an exercise designed to demonstrate the optical center of a page. It requires your participation. You'll need a pencil. Please put away your line gauge for a moment so that you're not tempted to use it.

Now, with your pencil, mark a dot in the blank rectangular box at left (Figure 34) where the center of the enclosed space seems to you to be. Don't measure it first. Do it by eye.

Finished? Now, get a line gauge or ruler and measure the distance from the dot you made to the top of the box. Calculate what percentage of the total space is above that dot as compared to the space below the dot. (The entire length of the box is 28 picas or approximately 4¾ inches.)

This is the formula to calculate that percentage:

$$\frac{\textit{Space above your dot}\text{ [your measurement goes here]}}{\textit{28 picas (4.75")}} = \frac{x}{100\%}$$

If the dot you drew happens to fall in the precise, mechanical center of the box—with 50 percent of the distance above and 50 percent below it—that is very unusual. Most people will place their dot approximately 45 percent of the vertical distance down from the top edge of the rectangle and 55 percent above its bottom edge. This is what appears to be the vertical center of the box.

Figure 34.

To a reader, the center of the page seems to be above its mathematical center. This point is called the *optical center* of a page. It is the spot at which the eye first rests when viewing a page.

The important thing to remember is the optical center of a page is above its mathematical center.

Proper Proportions

Though they could just as easily be made square, photographs, books, magazines and envelopes, are nearly always rectangular in shape. Also, they are all made into rectangles that have a marked difference of size in one dimension as compared to another. It's apparent at a glance that one dimension is significantly different than the other. The reason is that things which are exactly square, and shapes which have no easily recognized proportional relationship to their dimensions, are visually uninteresting.

From the examples in Figure 35, you can see that a rectangle having twice the length on one side that it has on the other, is not an especially pleasing shape either. The extremes are too great. The ancient Greeks—who held proportion to be the most important aspect of design—considered the most attractive proportions to be more than 1 to 2 and less than 2 to 3. That proportion is approximately 3 to 5 and is known as the golden proportion or golden mean.

In the publishing industry, the printer's oblong, with a ratio of 2 to 3, or the golden proportion, 3 to 5, have been the preferred proportions to use to create appealing document shapes. The vertical dimension doesn't always have to be the longest. An oblong page of 5 to 3 proportion, or a book of 3 to 2 proportions have equally pleasing shapes.

Often for convenience and economy, you'll be using standard paper sizes such as U.S. Letter Size, with approximately 2.3 to 3 proportions, or A4, which has 3.6 to 5 proportions. However, if you're establishing a size for your document other than these conventional ones, it's important that you give it interesting dimensions. Avoid using those awkward and amateurish proportions that are unappealing to readers.

The important things to remember here are that

Figure 35. Dimensions: Shape 1 has dimensions of no easily perceived proportional relationship; 2 is square, and 3 is twice as long as it is wide.

the shape of a page and the shape of things on the page itself, should not be exactly square; and the most pleasing proportions for these shapes are between 2 to 3 and 3 to 5.

Paper Page

The paper page is the size and shape of the document itself. The image you print on the paper page is called the *type page*. The type page includes the mass of type and art on the paper page (see Figure 36). But for size calculations, the type page does not include the page number or a small footer or header.

When designing pages, the idea is to create a paper page of pleasing proportions, then make the type page proportions agree with it.

Next, you'll need to decide on how much of the paper page will be taken up in type and artwork. In this way you calculate the total space given to margins.

The amount of space you allow the type page to occupy on the paper page varies with the publishing project. A small type page—meaning a page with extra wide margins—such as you'll find in a formal invitation, connotes luxury. The relatively small margins of a newspaper—the large proportion of the page given to type—implies commercialism. Most documents need margins that are somewhere in between these two extremes. In a typical publishing project, the type page will occupy about 65 percent of the paper page.

The next question is how to calculate the width and depth of a type page that will occupy 65 percent of the area of a paper page. This is accomplished by multiplying each dimension of the paper page by .8 for its corresponding type page dimension. For example, if you're using an 8½" x 11" page on which you'd like to have a type page size that equals 65 percent of the paper page size, multiply 8½" by .8 to get the width of the type page and multiply 11" by .8 to get its depth.

Convert the inches to picas first, then for con-

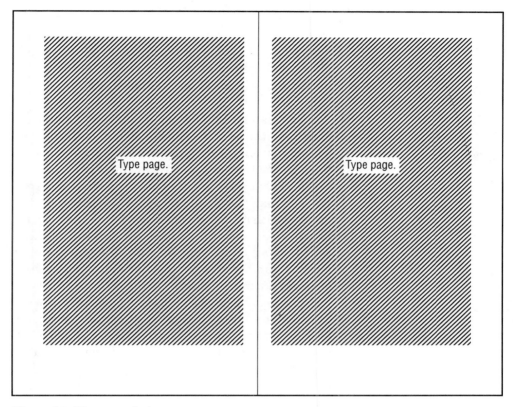

Figure 36. These two facing pages contain shaded boxes representing type pages occupying 65% of the paper page. This is figured by calculating 80% of width and depth of the paper page for type page size.

venience, round off your type page dimensions to the nearest pica.

If you're using expensive paper on a luxury publishing product, the type page should take up about 50 percent of the paper page or less. This will give a more formal and luxurious appearance to your project. Generous margins will also show off beautiful paper.

A type page using 50 percent of the paper page area is 70 percent of the paper page's width and 70 percent of its depth. In other words, multiply the paper page dimensions by .7 to find the appropriate type page dimensions.

By subtracting the type page width and depth from the paper page dimensions you'll find how much margin space must be allocated on your pages.

Margin Space

Since the optical center of a paper page is above its mathematical center and because type groups look best when they concentrate their visual weight above the center of their space, it follows that the type page should be positioned high up on the paper page.

The standard professional publishing method is to put two-thirds of the combined total of the top and bottom margin space in the bottom margin and one-third on the top margin, as shown in Figure 36.

If your project involves only one sheet of paper, the side margins should be equal to each other. For projects with more than one page, figure the margins in pairs of pages that face each other. These are called *facing pages,* and they are the pairs of even and odd numbered pages that open up together, such as pages 88 and 89 here.

For design purposes facing pages are always considered a unit. The inside, or center margins of facing pages combine visually, so each should be half the size of the outside margins of the page. This means the two inside margins combined—called the gutter—equal a single outside page margin (see Figure 36).

If a binding is going to be used that will take up part of the center margin of the paper page, allow space for it. Calculate inside margins only on the *visible* part of the page, not on any part that's going to be hidden when bound.

Shapes on the Page

As noted, the proportions of the type page should conform to those of the paper page. As much as possible, art on the type page should also agree with the paper page in shape. Since most pages are rectangular, illustrations, photos and other artwork should also be rectangular. Objects on a page may be upright, oblong or tilted, but they should maintain that rectangular character—this is the safe way to design your pages.

However, if you want to create contrast, as designers of newspaper and magazine advertisements

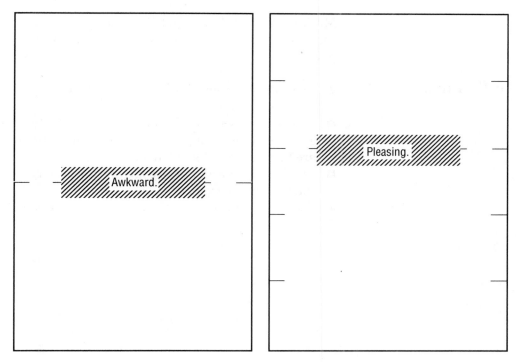

Figure 37. Left, small type group centered mechanically on page. Right, type group centered on its own and the page's golden proportion.

often do, a different shape added to a rectangular composition provides novelty and can concentrate attention. But if you're going to create contrasting shapes, go all the way. Make your circular shapes definite circles, not rectangles with rounded corners or merely wavy lines.

Small Type Groups

On many publishing projects, you must position a small type group or small piece of art on a page that will otherwise remain empty. Two common examples are the title page and the dedication page of a book. The mathematical center of the page is an unattractive position for these elements (see Figure 37).

To position such an element in an appealing way, find the object's golden proportion on its vertical dimension and center that on the golden proportion of the page. This is accomplished by finding the point on the object that is three-fifths of the distance from its bottom image edge to its upper image edge.

Mark that point. Then find the point on the page that is three-fifths from the bottom and align the two points.

In Summary

- The optical center of a page is above the mechanical, or measured, center of a page.
- The square is not a pleasing shape for designs. The most interesting proportions for publications are between 2 to 3 and 3 to 5.
- The bottom margin of a page should be larger than the top margin.
- Facing page inside margins are considered as one unit.

CHAPTER

Display Type

When set in type, the letters of our alphabet have an innate beauty that we often miss. We take for granted that which we see frequently, and with type, we focus on the message contained in the words. We don't necessarily look to the medium itself—the typeset letters—as a source of aesthetic enjoyment. This is appropriate. When type itself is noticed to be beautiful, it's usually because of the combination of form and function—the harmony of message and medium.

The practice of displaying type, when done well, is the process of showing off the inherent beauty of typeset letters in concert with a message. You can see many effective examples of displaying type in the advertisements in newspapers and magazines.

Purpose of Display

Displaying type is the process of varying type's size, slant, weight and arrangement based on the intended communication. By displaying type you prioritize elements, organize related items and funnel readers' attention through the main sections of your message. The effect is to help readers comprehend your message concisely and accurately and to leave them with a clear, persuasive impression.

The term *display type* is used to refer to large or prominent type as opposed to text-size type. Large type requires particular attention to its appearance and in turn, it can emphasize and enhance a message, and give infinite variety to your designs.

Just as some typewriter characters, such as neutral quotes and double hyphens, look inelegant when typeset, so too do some text-size typesetting conventions look inappropriate when applied to larger display-size type. For example, in large size type, double quotes (" ") appear too big and are unnecessary because you seldom need to denote quotes within quotes in these type sizes. Change double quotes into single quotes (' ') in display type. Also, as noted in chapter Five, substitute the shorter en dash for any em dashes in these large type sizes.

Kerning Type

Since each letter of the alphabet and each character of punctuation has a unique shape, its amount of surrounding white space is also unique. Look at how character shapes and their surrounding white space come together in these pairings:

LT Te ." db MN

In the first three pairs, the combined total of the white space between the characters is relatively high. In the last two pairs, there is relatively little total white space between the two characters.

Kerning type is eliminating excess built-in space between problem combinations of characters (see Figure 38). It minimizes distracting white space gaps within words, giving an even visual rhythm to the weight of the character strokes. This quality of type is referred to as even typographic color.

Pair kerning is carried out automatically, in a limited way, by professional-level desktop publishing programs. New programs are coming on the market that allow you to create your own kerning tables to do an even more effective job. But still, it's vital to have the ability to kern manually on your desktop publishing system.

Figure 38. Kerning.

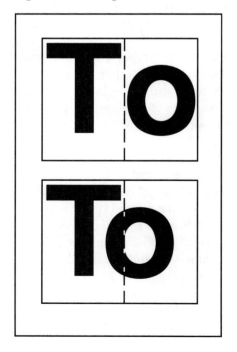

'We, the people ...'
Unkerned.

'We, the people ...'
Kerned.

Figure 39. Manually kerning lines of display type greatly enhances readability.

With large type it's especially important to kern because the gaps between problem pairs of letters are very obvious. When using display-size type, kern characters in a word relatively closely together so they visually have approximately equal letterspacing (see Figure 39). Characters should not actually touch though. An easy way to remember this is by the acronym TNT. It stands for Tight Not Touching. Kerning will darken up a line of display type and give it a customized, tailored look which is attractive and reads easily.

In text, kerning contributes to readability also, though text type needs to be a little more open than larger type. If you have the ability to set kerning values for your text type, remember that it should not be kerned as tightly as larger, display-size type.

Tracking Type

What's called tracking in desktop publishing programs is eliminating (or adding) the same user-specified amount of letterspacing between each character. Since it affects the same amount of space between each letter regardless of letter shape, it does not even out the white space between characters. It only reduces (or enlarges) the total amount between them.

Specifying a minus amount of tracking for type reduces the total amount of letterspacing. Minus tracking makes type appear darker, or bolder. Specifying a positive amount of tracking adds letterspacing and makes type appear less bold.

As with kerning, display type looks better when tracked more tightly than text-size type. Text type must be more open to avoid a dense, intimidating look. Be consistent in tracking text type. A paragraph tracked tightly next to one without tracking will appear to be much darker—it destroys the uniform look of your text.

Figure 40.

Typography is difficult to define but I know it when I do it ...

Second line mechanically centered.

Typography is difficult to define but I know it when I do it ...

Second line visually centered.

Spacing Adjustment When setting prominent and important lines of type such as headlines, and when designing business cards and letterhead, plan to spend some time visually adjusting the spacing between and around letters, lines, punctuation, and other characters. Pay special attention to kerning, to adjusting mechanically centered lines, to line spacing, and to wordspacing in order to give your type an even appearance. There is no software available to replace the human judgements involved here, and this is where the ability to adjust spacing manually is very important.

Center display type visually. Lines beginning or ending with punctuation have built-in space around them and so must be adjusted to make them appear visually centered. Generally this amounts to ignoring the punctuation and centering just the type (see Figure 40).

Lines composed mainly of figures appear to have less leading above them. Combining lines of upper and lowercase words with lines of numerals sometimes makes the line spacing appear to be greater between one line than the next. In these cases, adjust the line spacing optically by adding a point or a half-point of leading above the line composed of mainly numbers (see Figure 41, top).

Parentheses, brackets and hyphens must be raised up slightly when used with capitals because they are designed to be centered on the x-height of a typeface's lowercase letters. In some programs this is not easy to do, but when it's important, you can cut and paste those characters as separate text blocks and manually center them (see Figure 41, middle). Other programs allow you to specify an individual character's placement in relation to the entire line's baseline.

A page makeup program's wordspacing defaults can give you mathematically correct wordspaces, but ease of reading requires that wordspaces in prominent lines of type appear as nearly equal as possible. Therefore, more spacing can be added between pairs of words in which one ends and the other begins with an ascender because there is less natural space between those letters. Reduce the space between pairs of words in which one ends and the next begins with short letters and punctuation (see Figure 41, bottom).

Flaming Embers
1234 Forest Fire Way
Lodgepole, NV 56789
801-364-6501

Lines of composed of numbers appear to have less spacing above them. This sample has 1.5 points of extra spacing above the last line.

Mechanical.	**(PARENTHESES)**
Raised.	**(PARENTHESES)**
Mechanical.	**[BRACKETS]**
Raised.	**[BRACKETS]**
Mechanical.	**HYPEN-ATION**
Raised.	**HYPEN-ATION**

Parentheses, brackets and hyphens are designed to be centered on lowercase letters. They should be raised for caps.

Number 10 Downing St., Apt. 3
London, England SW1

Use less wordspacing after punctuation.

Figure 41.

Letterspacing Type

Letterspacing a line of type, such as a display line or a line of a logo, can lend emphasis and elegance to it. But in order to retain readability, follow these guidelines.

Set the type to be letterspaced in all capital letters because they are blocky and can accommodate extra space around them. Letterspacing lowercase weakens its design, making it inelegant to look at and difficult to read.

A COLLECTION OF LETTERS
Not enough extra wordspacing.

A COLLECTION OF LETTERS
Words are more easily distinguished here.

Figure 42. When letterspacing display type, insert twice as much extra space between words as you put between letters.

Always letterspace the entire line, not just a section of it.

When letterspacing metal type, the rule is to treat the wordspaces as letters. This means that you put the same amount of extra space on *both* sides of a wordspace as you put between the letters within a word. The rule holds true in desktop publishing as well. For our purposes, it amounts to adding twice as much *extra* space between words as you have between letters. If you don't do that, you'll end up with what looks like a collection of letters rather than a line of words (see Figure 42).

Once your letterspaced line is set, if the words still aren't readily distinguishable, add more wordspacing.

Cheat Leading

Cheat leading, also known as minus line spacing, is setting multiple lines of display-size type so that the baseline-to-baseline depth is less than the point size of the type used (see Figure 43).

Cheat leading darkens up a main headline and

Tight leading and tight kerning on a display line.

28 points

30-point Helvetica set on 28-point leading.

Figure 43. Display type often looks good cheat leaded, or set so that its leading is less than the point size of type.

lends emphasis to it. It's a useful technique when setting two or more lines of all capitals in large type because consecutive lines of all capitals, since they have no descenders, usually appear to be separated by a considerable white space gap.

Underlined Type is Difficult to Read

Though <u>Underline</u> is on the menus of most desktop publishing programs and is temptingly easy to use for emphasis, it actually reduces the legibility of the words underlined.

Readers recognize words by word shapes, rather than by putting letter combinations together. The underline rule, as formatted in desktop publishing software, makes major changes in the shape of words. It runs a relatively heavy rule just under the baseline of the letters, through the wordspaces and through the descenders. The combined effect makes even familiar words somewhat difficult for a reader to recognize.

This is one way to underline type and keep it readable.

Figure 44.

Provide emphasis and convey a sophisticated, readable look by underlining type with a fine rule—try using a half-point rule or less on smaller type. Don't run the underline rule through wordspaces and descenders (see Figure 44). It's a slow process to underline this way, but the result actually does add some emphasis to a word or phrase rather than reducing its legibility.

The Outline and Shadow options on desktop

publishing software Type menus are similarly crude and difficult to read. The best advice is to leave these programmed attributes unused.

Type Group Shape

With the professional page makeup software available for today's microcomputers, it's easy to set groups of type into virtually any shape. But even though type can be fashioned to fit unusual contours, care must be taken or its readability will suffer from extremes of line length, letter-spacing and wordspacing. Novelty of shape is pointless if it draws attention only to the type's arrangement and not to the message that the type is attempting to convey.

The following traditional arrangements of display type groups are both easy to read and familiar to readers. With all display type groups, position the largest display item within it, or the longest line, as close to the top as possible.

The Inverted Pyramid. One common mistake is to suppose that a type group on a page requires a foundation or a base underneath it. This is not so. Type looks best when suspended like a pendant on the page.

The inverted pyramid arrangement of type concentrates its weight above the mathematical center of its space and this is one reason why it's such an effective and well-used arrangement (see Figure 45).

A reader's eye tends to move toward the apex or point of a shape, so with the longest line at the top and shortest at the bottom, the reader's attention is pointed down into the text below. The inverted

No Other Hard Drive Stacks Up to Ours.

Greetings and Warmest Wishes for a
MERRY HOLIDAY
M O D E R N   D I S P L A Y   C O M P A N Y
Suite 41, 19011 West Highland Drive, Jackpot, Nevada 84104

This ad was built by a mouse and printed by a laser.

Figure 45. Top, inverted pyramid. Middle, squared up, or rectangular type group. Bottom, asymmetrical grouping.

pyramid's progressively shorter lines allow the reader to read out of the type group. A pyramid shape, starting with short lines of type and ending with long ones, requires more concentration because the reader must read into progressively longer lines.

Squaring-Up Type Groups. The rectangle is the standard shape for text type groups. It harmonizes with the shape of the paper page which itself is nearly always rectangular. It can be tricky to use as a shape for display type arrangements though. Here (see Figure 45, center), lines of type are squared up with each other on a common left and right margin. It's no problem if the copy happens fit well this way. Often though, a few of the lines will take too much letterspacing to square up with the rest.

Remember, if you do square up a type group with letterspacing, you should only letterspace lines of all capitals. Letterspacing lowercase display type results in a line that's very difficult to read.

Asymmetrical Grouping. Type that is not text does not necessarily need to be fit into symmetrical shapes. Usually lines of display type are more interesting to look at when they are unequal in length anyway, so type can be left to fill out lines as the thoughts expressed dictate (see Figure 45, bottom). Still, the main display element always should be towards the top, often you can transpose and rearrange lines to manage this.

In order to give an asymmetrical arrangement of display type balance, center each line.

In Summary

- Even out the spacing in important lines of type for an eye-catching appearance and easy reading.
- The most prominent element of a display type group should go towards the top.

CHAPTER 9

Page Layout

Every new publishing project poses different challenges in page layout and composition. Desktop publishing is an especially productive way to create and produce nicely designed pages because it brings all the elements of a page—text, headlines and art—together for preview and rearrangement.

An effective layout for a page or an advertisement will have a balance between uniformity and contrast. Too little contrast—too much uniformity—fails to arouse reader's interest. An example is a newsletter page composed entirely of text. A layout having too much contrast—too little uniformity—confuses readers with competing elements, exemplified by a page with many gratuitous graphic components. Balance your layouts so a reader is both invited to begin, and encouraged to finish reading the message.

A reader-accommodating design will visually organize information as well, arranging it into groups with a structure that makes relationships and important points obvious.

Thumbnail Sketch

Page makeup software won't propose an appealing layout based on the material that you need to publish, so it's most helpful to thumbnail sketch design possibilities before production begins. A thumbnail sketch is a drawing in miniature of a page layout that includes representations of all the essential page components—text blocks, headlines, photos and graphics (for an example of a thumbnail sketch, see Figure 46.)

The sketching process is creatively very helpful. Frequently alternate page arrangements suggest themselves by virtue of elements being drawn in relationship to each other. Unworkable ideas very quickly reveal themselves as well. By the time you bring up a blank page on your computer screen, the thumbnail sketches will give you a much better idea of the design prospects for each page.

These thumbnail sketches are for your own use, so precision is unnecessary. Instead of modifying, or revising an existing sketch, it's just as fast to throw it away and quickly draw a new one. For these reasons, a computer, even one with a simple paint-type program, is not an efficient tool for sketching layout ideas. Use paper and pencil.

Page Colors

In a newsletter, newspaper, magazine, tabloid and most periodicals, readers require lines of text that are generously leaded and column widths that are narrow enough to easily scan lines. Once you've set the copy with those highly readable attributes, the next problem arises: Pages of solid type are not interesting to look at nor inviting to read.

In laying out, it helps to look at a page as if it has three colors: Headlines and boldface type are black. Text is grey. The space around elements is white. For an inviting and balanced design, avoid congesting either the grey elements or the black elements on a page. Break up the solid grey areas of text into less formidable sizes, but in doing so, be careful not to concentrate dark artwork, headlines and other boldface type into one area.

White space is breathing room for a reader and provides contrast with the other colors on a page. Studies show that when given a choice, readers prefer a page with more white space over another version of the same page with less white space. Allow your readers plenty of breathing room.

Fig. 46.

Problem: Page composed of solid type makes it grey and uninviting to read.

Solution: Begin more stories on the page to allow readers several entry points.

Text should be broken up into eyefuls on a page. There are many ways to do this. You can insert photos, charts, graphs and other illustrations. By using both long and short stories on a page (see Figure 46), you will break up lengthy text blocks and at the same time allow readers another access point into a page. Often it requires continuing—or jumping—a long article onto a following page, but this is preferable to a page of solid text.

Another way to add contrast to large sections of text is the use of pullout quotes—quotations pulled out from the story and set in larger type. By choosing quotations with arresting, piquant content, you can arouse readers' curiosity while providing contrast to relieve the visual monotony of long text passages (see Figure 47).

Don't attempt to tell the whole story in a pullout. Short quotes look best and their content tends to be more provocative than longer ones, so take the liberty of editing pullouts for length.

On an 8½"x11" page with text of 9- to 11-point type, set pullout quotes in 12- or 14-point boldface or

Fig. 47.

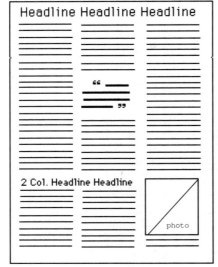

Quotations can be copied from a story, set larger and inserted into large grey areas of text. Also, pullouts can be set outside text to stimulate readers' interest.

18-point in the medium, or book (regular) italic. With a larger page size, the pullout quotes can be set larger.

Maintain Balance

As mentioned, you must balance between maintaining interest by avoiding visual monotony on one hand, and confusing readers with clutter on the other. Don't overuse art and other non-text elements. Further, place them thoughtfully so that the reader's train of thought is not suddenly interrupted and in such a way that widows aren't created in the text afterwards.

If an article is especially long, twelve inches or more, readers may hesitate to tackle it. One way to make it appear shorter is to position it horizontally on the page rather than vertically (see Figure 48). Instead of running it in one or two long columns going from the top of the page to the bottom, divide it evenly into as many columns as your page has and run the text under one headline across the page.

Effective design requires visually organizing related elements for the convenience and easy comprehension of your readers. The audience should be able to see at a glance what headlines, stories, pictures and graphics go together. Make a point of grouping all items that go with one story (see Figure 49, left).

One way to organize related items is to surround them with a border of white space that is obviously larger than the white space between items. Another way is to enclose related items within a box made of rules. Remember to leave adequate white space between the box and the elements inside it. The larger the box, the more space should go between the page elements and the rule. On even the smallest boxes leave at least one pica between the box and the elements in the box. White space in a layout should not be considered wasted space; it focuses reader's attention on the page elements.

Fig. 48.

Problem: Two long stories on a page. Uninteresting to look at and tedious to read.

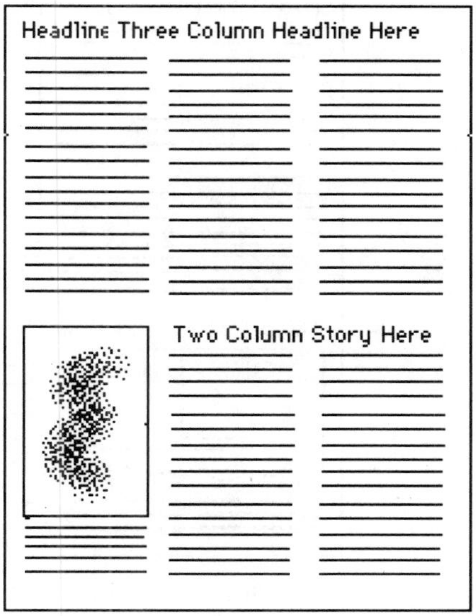

Solution: Arrange long stories horizontally to make them appear shorter. Add graphic.

Fig. 49.

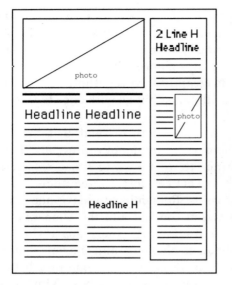

Organize related elements so readers don't have to guess what goes with what.

Cluster headline, story, caption when adding large amounts of white space to a page.

Fig. 50.

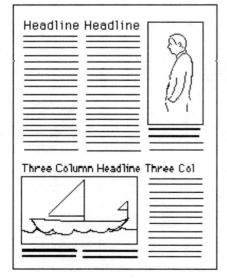

People in profile, or any art with direction, should not look or point off the page.

When adding large amounts of white space, add it to the outside of the page, *not* between headline and text or between photo and story. Always cluster headline, text and story (see Figure 49, right).

Generally speaking, each page of a periodical should include at least one photograph or other non-text element. This gives the reader's eyes something to focus on. The white space surrounding it gives readers breathing room and breaks up long passages of text as well.

The eye tends to follow the apparent direction of motion of an image, place pictures of people or things that seem to be pointing or moving so that they appear to be pointing into the page or into the text, not away from it (see Figure 50). Similarly, photos of people in profile should be arranged to appear to be looking into the page.

The size of a headline must be in proportion to the size of its story. The longer the story, the larger its headline may be. The largest headline should go at the top of the page and other headlines should decrease in size in proportion to the length of their

Fig. 51.

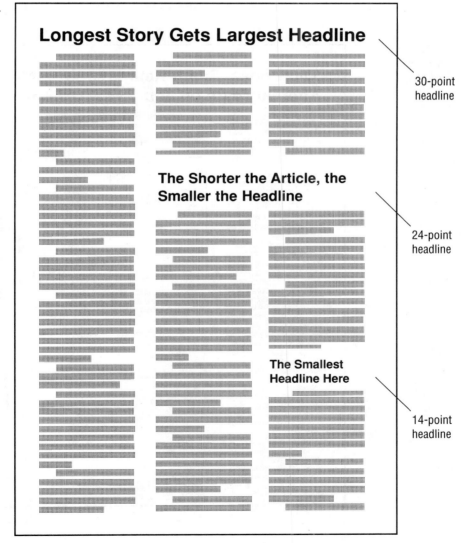

Longest Story Gets Largest Headline

30-point headline

The Shorter the Article, the Smaller the Headline

24-point headline

The Smallest Headline Here

14-point headline

stories and their distance from the top of the page (see Figure 51).

On a page size of 8½"x11" the largest headline should be no more than 30-point, otherwise it will look too large in proportion to the page.

Be careful not to place two unrelated headlines side by side on a page, this easily confuses readers (see Figure 52). Similar elements positioned this way are said to bump. Bumping unrelated photographs can cause the same kind of problem.

Fig. 52. Avoid bumping unrelated headlines.

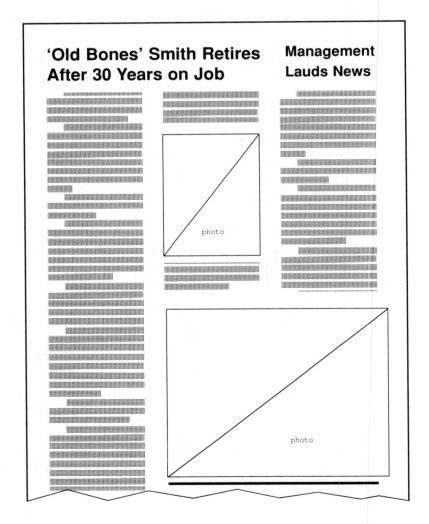

*Fig. 53.
Direction of
flow on a
page.*

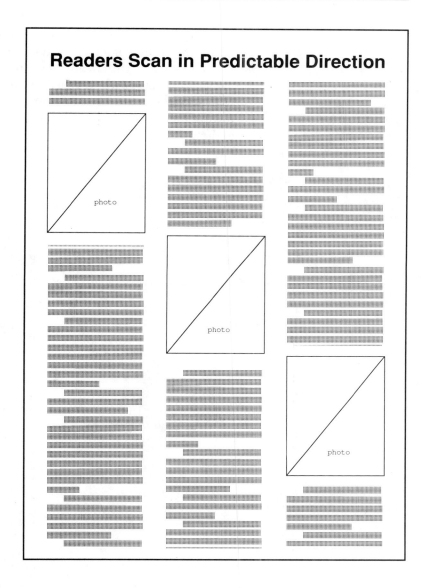

Readers tend to start reading a page from its upper left-hand side, then they scan diagonally down to the lower right-hand side. Layouts can take advantage of this normal direction of flow (see Figure 53) to usher readers through a document.

An effective technique for preventing over-crowded pages is to block with white space, meaning add large amounts of white space to one side or to the top or bottom of a page (see Figure 54).

While pages with too little white space are uninviting, poor use of white space can make them even worse. Never add large amounts of space *between* page elements, always cluster page elements together.

Fig. 54.
Blocking
with white
space.

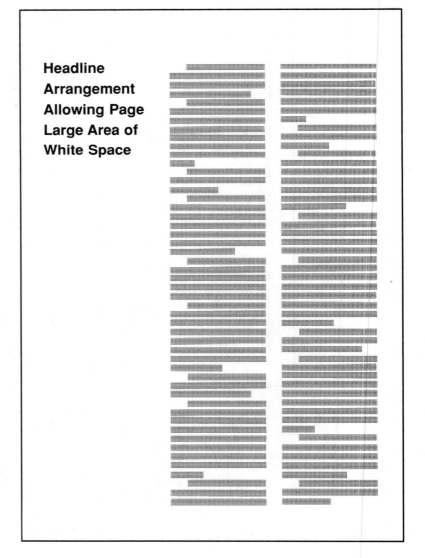

In Summary

- A good page layout balances contrast and uniformity. Pages of all text are not inviting to read, and pages with many competing graphic elements put off readers by confusing them.
- Always sketch layout ideas before trying them out in a page makeup program.
- Well-placed white space visually organizes a page, provides breathing room for readers, and focuses attention on other page elements.
- The eye follows the apparent direction of motion of an image. Position pictures of people to look into the page not off of it.

Display Ads

A display ad is an advertisement within a publication that is set off by a border and has various sizes and styles of type. As you learned in chapter Eight, the process of deciding upon and setting these various weights and arrangements of type is called displaying type. It provides emphasis, organization, and keeps the audience's eyes moving on the correct path throughout the message.

The most important thing to remember when creating a display advertisement is that your typical reader has the attention span of a *hummingbird* when it comes to reading advertisements. Whatever you create must be able to arrest the attention and arouse the interest of someone scanning ads on pages at a rate of seconds-per-ad.

For this reason, designing advertisements is a demanding craft. Even if you never attempt one yourself, the following principles apply equally well to many kinds of information presentation.

Readers' Interest

A reader's level of interest in an advertisement can be separated into three categories:

In Interest Level One, the reader scans the most prominent feature of the ad—usually a clever headline or arresting photo—is not interested, and goes on to look over the rest of the page upon which the ad is situated. Here, the Level One reader sees the ad's most obvious element and is not curious enough about it to continue reading the ad.

Figure 55.

The vast majority of readers of any display advertisement fall into this category.

In Interest Level Two, the reader scans the ad's most eye-catching element and is interested enough by it to glance at the second most conspicuous component of the ad. Generally, this is the advertiser's name and logo (symbol).

With a Level Two reader, an advertiser can gain some name recognition at least. The Level Two reader notices the ad and associates a sponsor's name with it.

The second most numerous amount of any ad's readers demonstrate this interest level.

In Interest Level Three, the reader sees the ad's most outstanding feature, is interested, reads the company's name, and then goes on to read the details contained in the remainder of the ad. The Level Three reader is the only kind of reader who will ever read any part of the advertisement other than the headline and company logo.

Within Interest Level Three are the fewest number of readers of any display advertisement.

WHEN YOU TRY TO EMPHASIZE EVERYTHING, NOTHING STANDS OUT. EFFECTIVE DISPLAY OF TYPE REQUIRES CONTRAST.

When you contrast lowercase with capitals, and boldface with book, the result makes a line **STAND OUT.** Effective display of type requires contrast.

Three Levels

The three levels of readers' interest dictate three display priorities. They are:

1. Headline
2. Company name
3. Further details

Size your advertisement's elements accordingly.

The most important component of your ad is the headline; it's the open door through which you entice readers into the rest of your ad. It must be interesting. If you don't rouse a reader's imagination here, he or she will never read the rest of your message.

A common mistake of novices is to make the

The Large Print Giveth *

This is the body copy. Generally, anything that is not the headline, the company name, or a graphic should be set here in paragraph form. Body copy will only be read by people who are comparatively very interested in your product or service. Don't try to emphasize it. Use a readable typeface in its regular weight.

 **Name of Company**

"Company's motto set in italic here."

Your Address and Phone Number Should Be Easily Accessible Here.

* And the small print taketh away. This six point type is a good size for disclaimers from your legal department.

Figure 56. Ad component proportions: the headline is the largest element, the company name is about three-fifths the size of the headline, and the rest of the message is set in text size and paragraph form as much as possible. One typeface family is used throughout the ad.

company name the most prominent part of an ad. It's unlikely though, that readers of a magazine or newspaper will be interested enough by reading a company name to go on to peruse the balance of an advertisement.

Concentrate on creating and displaying the headline because it determines your ad's effectiveness. The headline must hook the audience in, promising to give the reader something or promising to make the reader's life better in some manner. The word *free* is often used in ad headlines for this reason.

Write the ad headline from the perspective of what's important to your audience. A mortgage company's ad headline shouldn't emphasize home loans, it should offer the romance of a new home. Companies that sell lip balm don't advertise petroleum jelly, but *Lip Therapy,* for the same reason. This makes an enormous difference in arousing interest.

Ideally, the headline should be very brief— about six words is best. Any more than twelve words is too many—remember you're dealing with hummingbird-length attention spans. Place your ad's promise near the top of the ad to give it the highest visibility and to take advantage of the normal direction of readers' page scan: top to bottom, left to right.

Readers do tend to start reading at the top on the left-hand side of an advertisement and then scan diagonally downwards to the bottom right. Place the elements of your ad to take advantage of the tendency. Too many breaks in this expected directional flow may be enough to distract readers away from the ad.

The easier to read that you make the headline, the more people will read it. Set it large and kern it carefully. Pay special attention to its leading. Consider using minus line spacing for a two-line headline, never leave it on autoleading.

Make the headline as large as possible without severely condensing its width and without unbalancing a small ad. Use the boldface weight of typeface. Stay away from shadow type or any excessively ornate type that's difficult to read.

Ad Borders

Display ads always have borders. Sometimes the border is the edge of the page, as in a full page advertisement, other times it's just white space around the ad elements. If the border is a rule, then the larger the ad, the heavier the weight of the rule should be.

The larger the ad, the larger the margin of space between the rule and other ad elements. White space within the ad focuses the reader's attention on the ad's type and art, it's not wasted space. If you squeeze elements in near your border and eliminate the breathing room that white space provides, you produce a shoe-horned look that easily turns reader's attention towards an ad more inviting to read.

Make the minimum margin between border and ad elements one pica. That margin increases proportionately as your ad increases in size. For example, a half-page magazine advertisement should get at least a three pica, or half-inch margin.

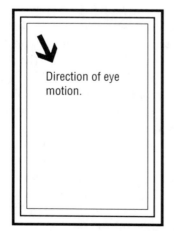

Direction of eye motion.

Figure 57.

Figure 58. Dots, points, and other border ornaments should be on the inside to stimulate eye motion toward the type.

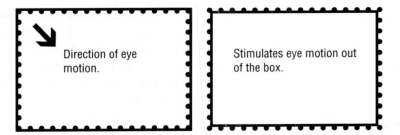

Direction of eye motion.

Stimulates eye motion out of the box.

It's important to take every opportunity to direct readers into your message and by design, some rule borders stimulate eye movement directionally. When using borders made up of parallel rules of different weight, the lighter rules should go to the inside because the eye tends to move from the heavy lines through the light lines. Dots, points, and other ornaments on a border should be on the inside for the same reason (see Figures 57 and 58).

Second Priority

A well-known company logo, since readers may recognize it without actually reading it, is a valuable element in a display ad. But whether you are using a logo and company name or just the logo, make it approximately three-fifths of the size of the main headline. If the headline is set in 42-point type, set the company name in 30- or 24-point type. This ensures that it's the second most prominent element of your ad and that it does not compete with, and distract attention from, the headline.

Put the company name and logo towards the bottom of the ad after the headline and after the smaller text. This way, Interest Level Two readers' must at least glance over the ad's body copy to get from the headline to it. You will have directed their eyes across the entire advertisement.

Third Priority

The rest of the ad—the details associated with your product or service—should be regarded as body copy, or text. It will only be read by people who are very interested and therefore highly motivated. It doesn't need emphasis, but it must be readable.

Organize as much as possible of this remainder

of the ad into text block and paragraph form. Group related elements. Avoid creating clutter or confusion that may draw attention away from the headline and company name. Make any disclaimers truly minute; the large print giveth, and the small print taketh away.

Superscript Dollars

Figure 59.

$\$39.99$	$\$39^{99}$
Without superiors.	With superiors.

When setting prices in 18-point type or larger, always make the dollar sign and the numbers representing cents superior (see Figure 59). A full-size dollar sign and full-size cents appear ponderous in large point sizes. Using superiors on either side of the numbers representing the dollars makes dollar figures stand out and also allows you to set them in a larger size.

Superior, or superscript positioning is available under the Position command of the Type dialog box in most page makeup programs.

Ad Typefaces

To avoid a busy look, use a maximum of two typeface families in an ad. One is often better. The best typefaces for display advertisements are ones that have black, bold and medium weights in regular widths and condensed widths. This allows a great amount of flexibility in both type weight and size.

Sans serif faces, because they have a contemporary look and are attention-getting, are the most appropriate choice for display advertisements. Helvetica, Avant Garde and Franklin Gothic are especially direct and forceful ad typefaces.

When you're finished setting an ad, print it out, look at it critically and ask: "What can I *de-emphasize* in order to have the headline and company name stand out even more?" This question is directed at attracting a greater number of Interest Level Two readers. Also ask, "What else can I do to standardize margins and group related elements in order to make the ad appear more organized and more inviting to read?"

Figure 60.

WORKMAN'S COMPENSATION
CLAIMS INVESTIGATED

All types insurance claims checked for validity
- **ALL SURVEILLANCE PUT ON VIDEO**
- **COURT TESTIMONY ALONG WITH VIDEO**
- **LOCAL REFERENCES AVAILABLE**
- **DAILY SURVEILLANCE REPORTS FAXED TO YOU**
- **NO ADDITIONAL FEE FOR VIDEO OR FAXING REPORTS**

We also handle civil and criminal cases that are unresolved.

CITY PRIVATE INVESTIGATIONS
000-0000

Workman's Compensation

CLAIMS INVESTIGATED

- All types insurance claims checked for validity.
- All surveillance put on video.
- Court testimony along with video.
- Local references available.
- Daily surveillance reports faxed to you.
- No additional fee for video or faxing reports.
- We also handle unresolved civil and criminal cases.

City Private Investigations
000-0000

In the top ad, the designer has tried to emphasize too many points and has not organized information for the reader. The result is both dull and confusing. In the redesigned advertisement below, one main point stands out. The bullets (dots) and white space help to group subordinate points. Greater variation in size and weight of the type provides emphasis.

Figure 61.

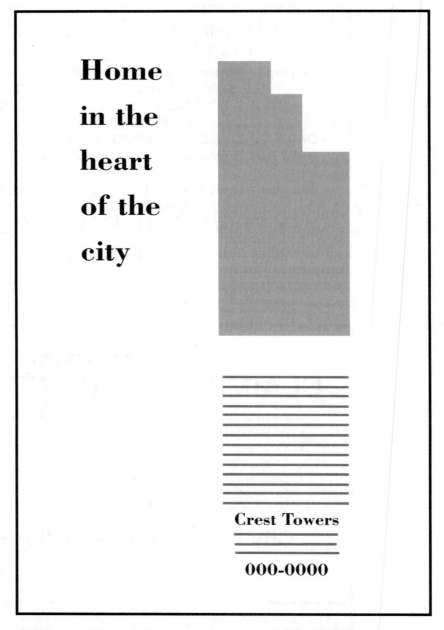

With the generous use of white space you can punctuate an advertisement. White space provides emphasis by making other ad components stand out. It also unifies elements of the advertisement.

Figure 62.

Don't use dingbats (ornaments) just to fill up space. Use them to provide direction or as eye-catchers. Dingbats must harmonize with the rest of the composition. For instance, don't use old fashioned-looking dingbats with a modern-looking typeface.

Figure 63.

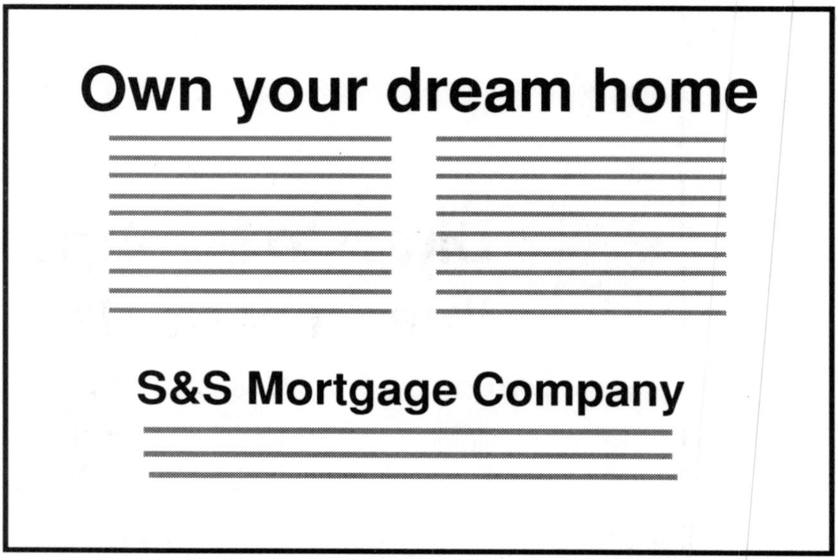

Own your dream home

S&S Mortgage Company

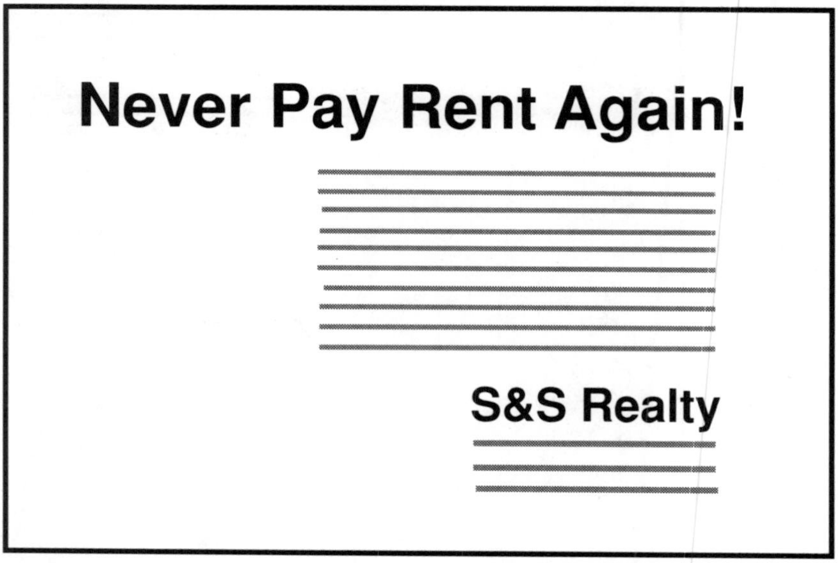

Never Pay Rent Again!

S&S Realty

The formal balance in the advertising layout above, is static suggesting quiet repose and harmony. Informal balance in the layout below suggests movement, arousing readers to action.

Figure 64.

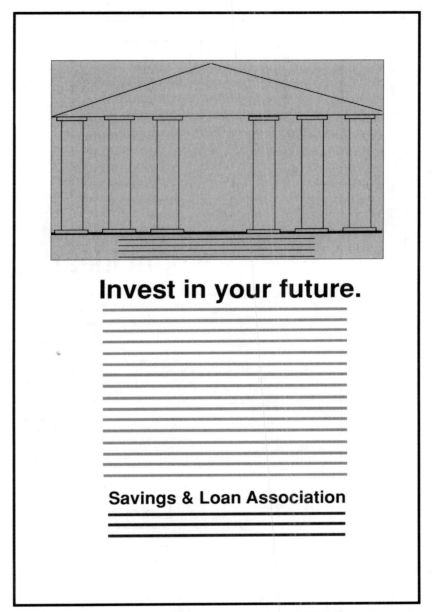

Invest in your future.

Savings & Loan Association

Formal balance in a layout is especially appropriate when you are attempting to convey a sense of stability and security important to many industries.

Figure 65.

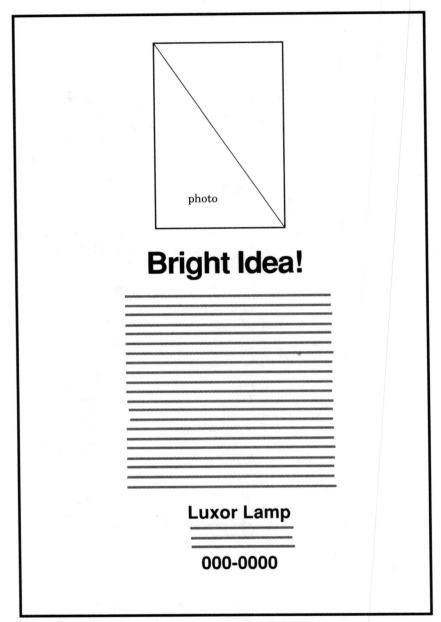

To add movement to a centered and formally balanced advertisement, shift the elements. The size proportions between headline, company name and body copy remain the same.

Figure 66.

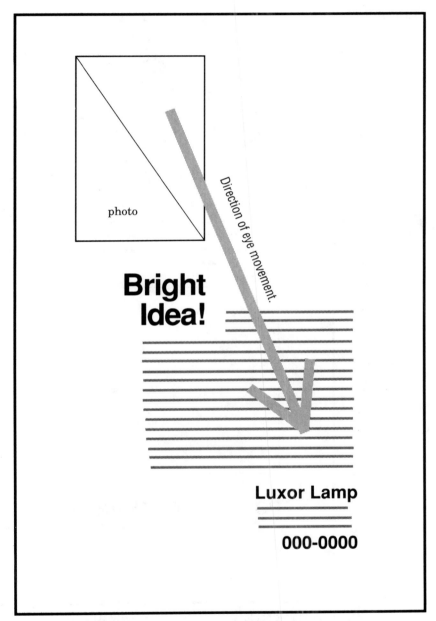

In this example, moving the elements provides an informal balance that harmonizes with the normal eye flow through an advertisement.

Figure 67.

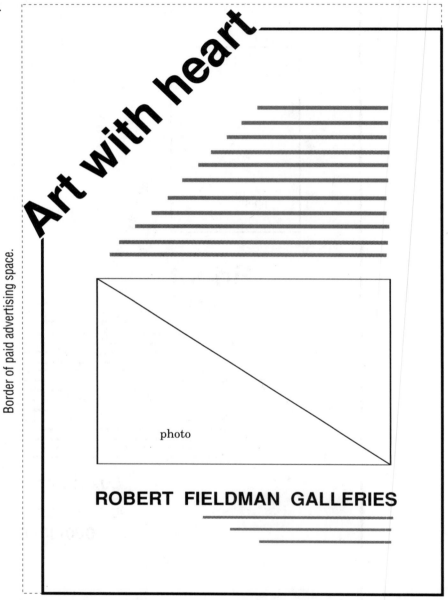

Border of paid advertising space.

Art with heart

photo

ROBERT FIELDMAN GALLERIES

Breaking into the border with artwork can be an effective way to add interest, movement and an inviting look.

Figure 68.

Border of paid advertising space.

Measure the whole image area of your advertisement, not just the rule border, to ensure that its size fits a publisher's specifications.

Figure 69.

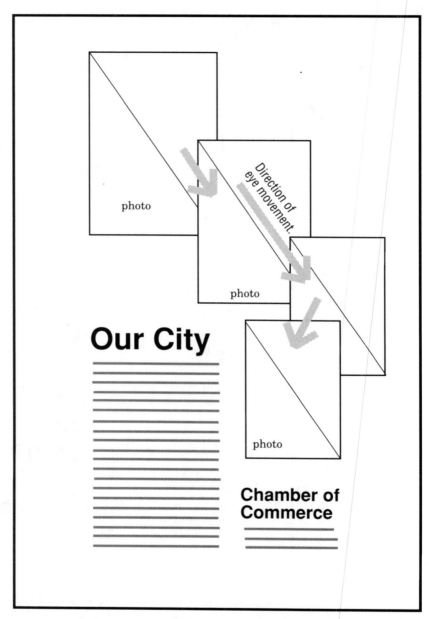

Your design should direct readers' attention through the advertisement by the thoughtful placement of art and white space.

In Summary

■ People only read an advertisement if they are hooked in by the headline or by an arresting photo.

■ All other components of an advertisement must be subordinated to the headline. The headline must promise, or offer the reader something.

■ If you try to emphasize everything, nothing stands out.

■ Use borders of a design that stimulate eye motion into the advertisement.

■ Use a maximum of two typeface families in an advertisement.

■ Visually organize, or group related elements.

CHAPTER **11**

Presentation Graphics

The three types of presentation graphics are overhead transparencies, slides and handouts.

Overheads are an informal presentation method and   because they can be printed directly from laser printers, its especially easy to create them on desktop publishing systems. Overheads are inexpensive to produce and you don't have to turn the lights out to show them.

Slides give you large size and rich colors, and so can have great impact. Usually no dialog with the audience is possible during a slide presentation, and since you have to turn the lights out, showing them is not a casual event.

Handouts are put together like books or proposals. They can either follow the projected presentation exactly, or reveal in-depth information that's too lengthy or too involved for the main body of the presentation.

Often business users purchase a particular presentation graphics program on the basis of exotic special effects that it can produce for slides, overheads and handouts. The purpose of a presentation though, is to communicate complicated ideas simply. A good example is the way an effective graph turns complex numerical data into an easily-understood picture. A sale depends upon your audience walking away both informed and convinced. By injudicious use of the extensive variety of typefaces, type attributes, clip art, screens, and colors available, you can obstruct rather than enhance communication. It's easy to go too far by creating competing visual elements that confuse, rather than inform, a viewer.

To be convincing, presentation graphics must be fitting to the product or service and to the audience. What's appropriate is a difficult question. Software salespeople can't move programs by talking about simplicity and good taste in presentations. They promote graphics using adjectives such as *eyepopping*. *USA Today* has used a bar graph made out of tall and short baby bottles to depict birth rate information. Similarly, a pie chart for a construction company's earnings might be created using a building outline to represent the whole; sections of the structure are then made to represent income from various sources. Is obvious symbolism suitable for your purpose, or is it too cute? How does one avoid going overboard with all the tools to do so very close at hand?

Plan First

Begin with a plan. Have a complete outline of what you want to say before you begin to create individual elements.

The most important part of presentation preparation is deciding upon just one primary idea with which to leave your audience. State it in a dozen words or less. When you've clearly articulated your theme, the time and relative emphasis on all other parts of the presentation must be subordinated to it.

Draw thumbnail sketches of each graphic in their proper sequence before you begin producing the graphics. This a storyboard and it is the place to decide upon the size, style and location of all of the main elements of each graphic or slide. Keep them uniform all the way through. In fact, be simple and consistent in using all graphical elements. It's easier to deliver a message clearly that way.

Consider the amount of information your audience can absorb. If you have information that requires much explaining, break it down and present it in smaller pieces. Size depends upon the kind of presentation and the data. For instance, during a slide presentation the audience doesn't have time to ponder a graph with a dozen series. In a handout however, a graph can be more complex because the reader doesn't have to comprehend it as quickly.

Make your design appropriate to your subject. If your theme involves clothing fashions, your layout and graphics can be more lively than if you're selling conservative utility company bonds.

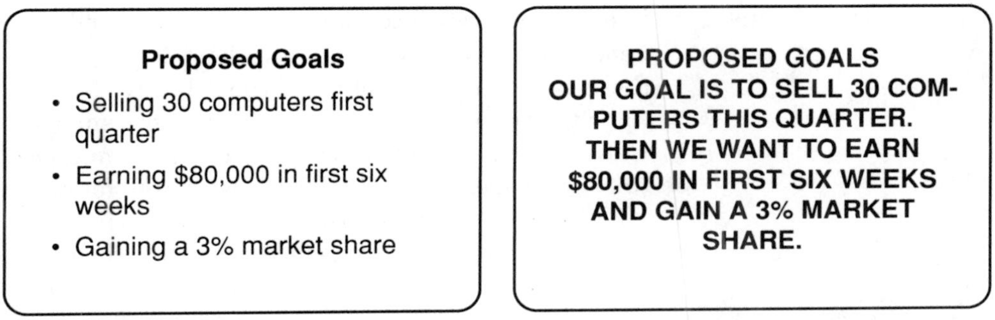

Figure 70. For slides, a few short lines begun with bullets works better than a paragraph.

Proposed Goals

• Selling 30 computers first quarter

• Earning $80,000 in first six weeks

• Gaining a 3% market share

PROPOSED GOALS OUR GOAL IS TO SELL 30 COMPUTERS THIS QUARTER. THEN WE WANT TO EARN $80,000 IN FIRST SIX WEEKS AND GAIN A 3% MARKET SHARE.

Text with Impact

As discussed in chapter Two, lines of all capitals are more difficult to read than lines of lowercase. Use lowercase letters as much as possible in presentations.

Set type flush left. It's easier for the reader to find the start of each line if they are lined up evenly on the left hand side against the margin.

Be brief, present one point per slide. A few short lines of bulleted information work better than long lines or paragraphs. (Bullets are large dots at the beginning of lines in a list that look like this: •.) For slides, use 6 or 7 words per line and a maximum of 6 or 7 lines per slide.

Visually organize the information—group related points together after one bullet and insert a blank space between them. Use the same size, style, and shape bullet at the start of each main item (see Figure 70).

Don't confuse viewers by changing styles. For instance, apply the same method of capitalization, and sentence structure throughout. Your lists can be either all phrases or all complete sentences. Don't mix them. Start out each point with the same part of speech, such as:

- Selling 30 computers this quarter
- Earning $80,000 in the first six weeks
- Gaining 3% in market share

For color presentations, employ the same color bullet all the way through.

Sturdy Typefaces

Use only one typeface family. For contrast and emphasis mix its bold, italic, and bold italic. Apply these variations sparingly and consistently.

Sturdy typefaces of simple design, such as Helvetica, Franklin Gothic, Lubalin Graph and Optima (see pages 48, 50, 52, 56, 57) work well for presentations. The particular virtues of these typefaces are that they will stand up to both slide making—where type is first extremely reduced to 35mm film, then projected to great size—and to low resolution printing. These families won't lose serifs and they have enclosed white spaces (counters) that don't fill in, even when set small. Typefaces with strongly contrasting thick and thin strokes, such as Bodoni (see Figure 71) or any typeface with delicate serifs reproduce poorly in these circumstances.

Text slides are easiest for viewers to read if you use a dark blue background with yellow or white words. Employ color for emphasis rather than type size. Warm colors, yellow, orange and red attract. Decide what colors you'll use, then apply them consistently from one slide to the next.

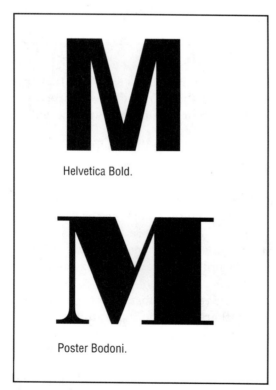

Helvetica Bold.

Poster Bodoni.

Figure 71.

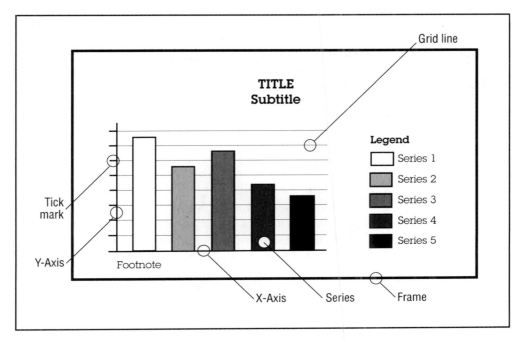

Figure 72.
Elements of
graphs.

During slide presentations, your audience will be sitting quietly in a dark room and too many text slides in a succession will tire them. Intersperse your text slides with graphic slides.

Simplify Data

The purpose of a graph is to show numerical data pictorially. The advantage of using a graphic is that it simplifies complex information.

The kind of graph to use depends upon the data you're presenting, but no matter what type of graphing technique you employ, eliminate nonessential elements. All graphs must have a title, but components such as subtitles, footnotes, grid lines, borders and legends are sometimes optional. If any of these items are not important to communicating the message, leave them out and you'll avoid clutter that competes with your point. For example, don't use a shadow box for each graph simply because the software automatically gives it one.

Showing trends, instead of exact numerical amounts is often the most effective way to present data. Round off large numbers and keep other details to a minimum. Grid lines behind line and bar charts are often superfluous. Use them only if you need to show the precise intersection of data and value.

Simplify by consolidating information. For instance, if you have several thin slices of secondary importance in a pie chart, combine them into a single slice and call it *Other*.

Don't add more than one or two annotations or explanations on any graph. If a graph needs extensive explanation, break it down into several separate charts with less information on each. If you attempt to tell the entire story including details, you may as well write an essay. For example, in a slide presentation use a maximum of five series of data in each bar or line chart. If you must show more series, break them down into several charts. Create a handout for your audience with all of the series included, which they can peruse later.

Extend the principle of design consistency to the size and shape of graphs. Create charts and graphs to the same dimensions when possible and locate them on the same area in each slide.

Use of Color

Employ color to denote relative significance. As with text slides, use warm colors such as yellow, orange and red, for emphasis.

Color also provides continuity. For instance, a certain year, product or category may be the same color throughout your presentation. Use a bright color to emphasize one series in a chart and then use lighter shades of the same color for the rest of the series. Using a separate primary color for each series is overdoing it.

Avoid busy, intricate patterns for the fills of your graphs in black and white presentations, they clash and tend to reproduce poorly. The weight of fills should be progressive between series. For example, use a solid white fill on the first series, then a light dotted or slanted line pattern, then darker patterns from left to right. Finish with a solid black series and you will have a configuration that's attractive to the eye.

In Summary

- First, decide on the one primary idea you want to communicate to your audience.
- Use a consistent style of type, color, bullet and layout throughout.
- Use color instead of size for emphasis.
- The purpose of a graphic is to simplify complex ideas.
- Eliminate all nonessential elements in a graph.

CHAPTER

Production Problems

In your quest to produce high quality documents from a desktop publishing system, you'll encounter many problems that are as old as printing itself. The challenge of ensuring the accuracy and quality of your publication's content—proofreading—is a major concern. Spell-checking and grammar-checking programs provide assistance here, but no substitute exists for carefully examining the page printouts.

Another traditional concern is for your *masters*—the camera-ready pages you create and from which your printer will make printing plates. Great care must be taken to ensure that these camera-ready pages are clean and extremely legible because their quality will determine the maximum print quality of the final product.

With each stage of reproduction in the printing process—master to negative, negative to press printing plate, plate to ink and paper—a discernable amount of quality is lost from the original. The more you economize on any production steps, the more the quality of the final product is compromised. You can easily see this in catalogues and magazines printed on rough, absorbent paper such as newsprint. Here small, light type is broken up or blurred, photos are somewhat muddy and often rules are not crisp, even if the camera-ready pages from which they're printed are quite good.

Setting white type on a black background and

setting black type on a grey background, in a manner that's easily readable in the final product, is tricky. It too provides a continuing design challenge for which you must be prepared.

New quality hurdles occur as well. The low resolution of laser printers—compared to most professional publishing systems—is one of them. While excellent for viewing the final composition and for proofreading, 300 dots per inch (DPI) resolution severely restricts your design choices in type size, type style, rules, screens, other design elements, and in the choice of paper for your document. The increasing availability of higher resolution output devices is a blessing for desktop publishing.

Low Resolution

Camera-ready copy is the final page from which the pressperson will actually make a printing plate. When you print out this camera-ready from laser printers, type's clarity is a special problem in sizes of less than 10-point type. At 300 DPI, there just aren't enough dots per character, in these small type sizes, to give letters acceptable legibility. Serifs blur or disappear, curves are wobbly and small counterforms— white space enclosed within letters—fill in. Later in the printing process when paper meets ink, more type clarity is lost.

Non-PostScript laser printer typeface designs have especially poor legibility in small sizes. PostScript typefaces look somewhat better at low resolution because they contain computer programming hints especially for the purpose of making the small point sizes print more clearly and so they have less noticeable distortion of form.

If you use 300 DPI laser printer output as camera-ready copy, remember that it's not possible to convey type design subtleties at these low image resolutions. Use medium weight typefaces of simple design on nine-point type and under. Very condensed, very bold and very light typefaces have especially compromised legibility in small sizes at low resolution. Also, there is a high minimum width to a type character's lines in low resolution. For instance, Helvetica Light comes out with nearly the same boldness as Helvetica Regular (Book).

Therefore, it's best to avoid using smaller than 10-point type when printing from 300 DPI masters. When you can't avoid it, use a typeface with a large x-height, little contrast between thick and thin strokes, and either no serifs or blunt serifs. Helvetica, Optima, Lubalin Graph and Franklin Gothic (see pages 48-50, 52, 56, 57) are examples of typefaces with these characteristics.

Another problem with using laser printer output for your printing masters, is that the end product looks particularly blurry when printed on smooth, or coated paper. For best results from laser printer masters, print the final product on paper that's slightly absorbent and has no smooth finish.

High Resolution

If you run out your camera-ready copy from a high resolution output device such as the Linotype Linotronic in at least 1,000 DPI resolution; *and* if you print to a good quality of paper, then six-point type is quite legible. But again, for best results with tiny type, use a typeface with a medium weight, and with a large x-height such as Helvetica and Optima, so letters will not fill in. Don't use typefaces with delicate serifs such as Bodoni, because the serifs will disappear in the reproduction process, giving the typeface a wholly new and completely unacceptable look.

If you have small type on high resolution camera-ready pages and you print onto cheap, highly absorbent paper such as newsprint, you'll find many of the same legibility problems that you encounter when printing small type from low-resolution camera-ready pages onto any kind of paper.

Screens Over Type

Overprinting black type on a screen can be attractive if the screened background is not very coarse, not too dark and provided that the type is bold enough to read easily.

Screens are course or fine depending upon how many dots per square inch make them up. This dots-per-inch measure is called *lines per inch* (LPI). The more lines per inch a screen has, the finer, or more capable of detail, the screen is and the smaller the dots are (see Figures 73 and 74). This characteristic of screens is different than the screen percentage, where a 100 percent screen is solidly reversed and a 50 percent screen is half white and half black, like a checkerboard. It's the screen percentage that is on the Shading menu of page makeup programs.

A coarse screen background is one where the individual dots making up the screen are large, easily visible and interfere with the readability of the type. Most newspapers use a relatively course screen of 65 or 80 LPI, depending upon their press and paper limitations. They print on coarse and absorbent paper, so finer screens—more dots per inch—will spread and fill-in when heavy, or will disappear completely if light. For a professional look, use screens of no less than 65 lines per inch.

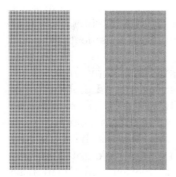

Figure 73. From left to right: screens of 65, 80 and 100 lines per inch. All are thirty percent.

Glossy magazines, because they print on high-quality coated paper, use 133 LPI screens. In order to do it well, they create the screens and type separately. The screen is directly exposed onto negative film which is then exposed onto the printing plate. This direct-to-printing plate process avoids aggravating the problems of reproducing tiny dots.

The only way for you to get consistently good quality from 133 LPI screens is to provide your copy to the printer in film negative form, and then print your publication on a high quality of paper. If you can't provide negatives, don't use screens of more than 100 LPI on your high-resolution camera-ready copy. The extra step of turning this reflective copy

Figure 74.

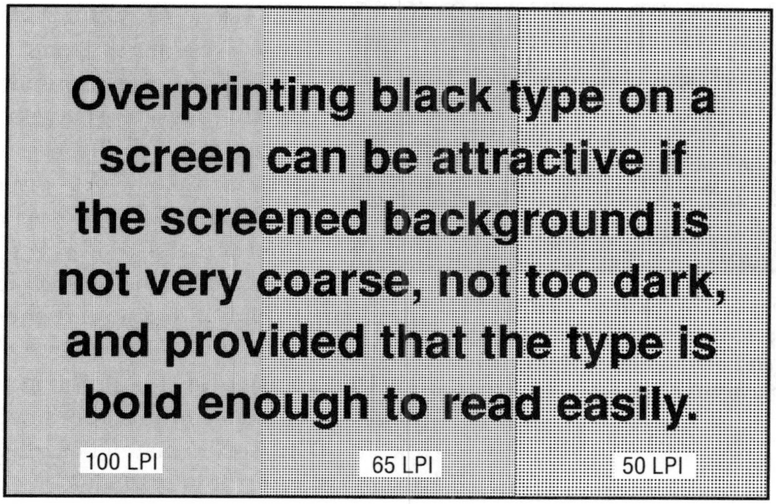

Overprinting black type on a screen can be attractive if the screened background is not very coarse, not too dark, and provided that the type is bold enough to read easily.

100 LPI   65 LPI   50 LPI

into a negative will render an uneven 133 LPI screen.

Crisp 100 LPI screens generally aren't possible to create from a laser printer, so you'll have to keep to 65 LPI screens on camera-ready you produce from these low resolution printers.

The larger and bolder the type, the darker you can make its overlying screen. In all but the largest type sizes, a 30 percent black screen (from the Shading menu) is the darkest that you can safely print over type without making it too difficult to read.

Reverse Type

When you reverse type, its readability is diminished. Studies show that white type on a black background is more difficult to read than black type on a white background. However, if you do reverse type, always use a bold weight or at least a medium weight typeface because blocks of black ink tend to fill in the fine lines of light weight typefaces, making words even more difficult to read (see fig 75). Set serif type in reverse no smaller than 10-point because serifs will fill in and disappear when reversed in small sizes.

A large black reversed area on a page that also

12 point Helvetica Bold

12 point Helvetica Book

12 point Helvetica Light

Figure 75. Bold or medium weight faces are easier to read on a black or solid color background.

has areas of regular black-on-white text type presents a special offset press problem. If the pressperson puts enough ink on the page to give you a solid, dark reverse, it's usually too much ink for the regular text, which will darken and start to fill in. If the pressperson sets the ink appropriately for the text, the reversed area will come out too light. Minor press adjustments can be made, but the result is usually less than perfect.

One solution to this problem is to screen down the reversed area so that it does not require as much ink. In other words, instead of solid black, make the reverse a 70 or 80 percent black screen. Remember to make the screen heavy enough so that the white letters are still easily read.

Proofreading

With the pressure of deadlines, you may not have enough time to proofread your pages before you send them to the press. No problem—but you will make time to *re-do* them when some unacceptable mistake is found after printing. By then of course, it's twice as late and twice as expensive.

You never actually save time by rushing through or (perish the thought) eliminating proofreading. It'll cost you time, money and it will hurt your reputation when you have to apologize or reprint.

Since the user takes on so much responsibility for the final product when desktop publishing, proofreading is especially important. When fewer people are necessary to create the pre-press product, there are not as many eyes checking things and often problems are not spotted before they are immortalized in ink.

The consequences of inadequate proofreading can be embarrassing. One newspaper ran a full-page paid advertisement with the main headline dropping the *r* in the intended *Shirt* Sale.

What a difference one letter can make!

Problem Areas

As readers, we recognize words by their shapes, not by putting combinations of letters together. We become accustomed to recognizing words in small, text-size type set in lowercase. When we see words set in all capitals or set in extra large sizes, it's very easy for the visual recognition process to fail. This is why errors in lines of prominent display type and in large prices are especially likely to escape detection during a cursory inspection. Professionals proofread words syllable-by-syllable sounding them out completely, and they always check headlines and prices *twice.*

In English, one letter or one combination of letters can represent more than one sound. Additionally, English comes from so many sources through the centuries, that it *teems* with spelling eccentricities. Becoming a good speller is a matter of checking the dictionary often. When proofreading, always have access to a dictionary.

Spell-checking and grammar-checking programs are very helpful. You should run your text through them before you proofread it. But these programs are often not able to detect a wrong word being used; or to reveal embarrassing *double entendres;* to grasp many errors in grammar; or to discover when copy is missing. It's important to keep a careful watch specifically for these problems when proofreading.

Make sure you proofread *all* last-minute copy changes. Typographical errors are especially apt to find their way into your pages from those frantic final modifications. Another point worth remembering: Because people tend to miss their own typing errors when proofreading, it's important that at least one person other than the typist, proofread everything.

Spacing Defaults

Any professional-level page make-up program will allow you to establish wordspacing defaults, also called wordspacing attributes. This is a trial-and-error process that involves printing out lines of type

and measuring the wordspaces in them and then
adjusting the defaults as necessary. Once you have
set defaults for maximum readability based on industry standards (see chapter One), you shouldn't
have to bother with it again. Hopefully, the default-
setting interface for your system is in percentages,
so that if you adjust defaults using 12-point type, the
proper proportions will carry through for all of your
type sizes.

Here's how to determine wordspacing values in order to set your defaults:

Set a few dozen lines of type flush left and
ragged right using a proportional (not monospaced) sans serif, 12-point typeface. Use 12-
point type to simplify the math involved. Use
sans serif type because it's easier to measure between words than is serif type. Also set a few
dozen lines of justified type on a line width of
about 15 picas, in that same typeface and size.
Type a typical mix of both short and multi-syllable
words.

Print out your lines from a laser printer or a
phototypesetter and look at the ragged right copy.
The wordspacing should be three-em, or 33 percent
of the type size, throughout. Since you're using 12-
point type, that would be 12 points divided by 3—4
points. With your line gauge (you *do* have a line
gauge now, don't you?) measure some of the
wordspaces in your copy to see if they are, in fact,
four points wide. Adjust your program's defaults if
necessary.

In justified copy the place to measure what the
desired default setting is now set on, is in the last
short line of any paragraph. It should also measure
out to four points of space—a three-em space in 12-
point type.

Next, find the justified line with the least
amount of wordspacing. That wordspacing should be
no smaller than a five-em space, which is 20 percent
of the point size being used—12 divided by 5. The
answer here is 2.5 points wide.

Wordspacing

For **ragged** copy: 3-em

For **justified** copy:
5-em Minimum
1 em Maximum

Figure 76.

Ideally the widest desired wordspace in the justified copy should be no larger than one em space, but flexibility here is allowable.

In Summary

- Avoid using smaller than 10-point type from low resolution printers as camera-ready copy.
- When reversing type from a black background, or when setting black type on a grey screen, set it in boldface.
- When printed from a high resolution output device, screens for overprinting type should be of about 100 lines per inch and they should be no heavier than 30 percent.
- Always proofread thoroughly.

Summary

The more interesting to look at and easy to read your document is, the more often it will be read. Your publications compete with professionally-designed documents and today's reading public is very busy. For these reasons, your design should organize and prioritize information, then present it in an easily-read format.

Spacing

To make type easy to read, the spaces between words always must fall within certain established parameters. The preferred amount of space between words of capital and lowercase letters is 33 percent of the point size of the type used.

Words typeset in lines of ALL CAPITALS are more difficult to read than words set in lowercase letters. Use lowercase letters whenever possible.

Pay attention to the line lengths of your type, especially in text. Keep a moderate amount of words per line—don't make your lines very long or unnaturally short. Adding leading between lines of text greatly enhances its readability.

Type Classification

Typefaces are categorized into a half-dozen design classifications. Choosing a suitable typeface for a specific purpose depends upon selecting from within the appropriate classification for the functions it must perform.

Roman typefaces have serifs and are the most appropriate typefaces in which to set large amounts of text. Roman oldstyle and transitional typefaces are particularly readable typefaces for text.

When selecting two typeface families to use together in a publication, choose families from different classifications. They should harmonize in design and shape. Using typefaces from three families in one publication can easily give your design a cluttered look.

Many guidelines you may have learned as a typist don't work well in typesetting. Convert double hyphens to em or en dashes, neutral quotes to true typeset quote marks, and inch marks to apostrophes and opening single quotes. Use one wordspace between sentences. Using two wordspaces between sentences leaves rivers of white space in text.

Design Simply

Design simply using type, rules, and illustrations in their abundant combinations. Use screens, ornaments and clip art sparingly. Though your desktop publishing system is capable of adding many exotic attributes to type and art, employ them only if they make a vital contribution to your message.

Always maintain a consistent text style—typeface family, size, and leading—throughout your publication.

The square is not a pleasing shape for pages or page elements. Use a rectangle of between 2 to 3 and 3 to 5 proportions.

The optical center of a page is above the mechanical (measured) center of a page. Center objects on a page visually—not mechanically.

Display type is large, prominent type. Display type groups don't require visual support underneath, they look best hanging in an inverted pyramid arrangement with the main element towards the top.

Page and Ad Layout

Look at your black-and-white page design as if it has three colors: Black, grey and white. Avoid congesting either black elements or grey elements. Be generous with white space, it is breathing room for the reader and provides necessary contrast for other graphic elements. Visually organize—cluster and group—related elements.

When designing display ads, hook readers with a brief promise in the headline or illustration. All other advertising elements must be subordinated to that main element.

Production

When creating camera-ready copy from a 300 DPI laser printer, avoid using smaller than 10-point type and use screens of 65 lines per inch.

When reversing type from a black background, or when setting black type on a grey screen, set it in boldface.

When printed from a high resolution output device, screens for overprinting type should be of about 100 lines per inch and they should be no heavier than 30 percent.

Always proofread thoroughly.

Practice safe computing.

Do your publishing well and have fun with it!

Glossary

Art
Anything on a page that is not type or white space.

Ascending letters
Letters such as lowercase *b, d, h,* and *l* which have components that protrude above the mass, or x-height, of the lowercase letters. That part which actually rises above the x-height is known as the ascender.

Baseline
An imaginary line running along the lower edge of type's x-height upon which the bottom of letters align.

Body
The space that the face of a letter of type is situated upon. Its height is measured in points and is called the type's *point size.* The body goes approximately from the top of the capital letters—or the top of the ascenders—to the bottom of the descenders.

Bullet
A large dot used to direct attention to the beginning of a line. A bullet looks like this: •.

Camera-ready copy
Finished artwork from which the printer will make a printing plate. Also called *master* or *artboard,* its quality will determine the maximum print quality of the final product.

Capitals
Uppercase letters.

Character
Letters, numbers, and punctuation.

Cheat leading
Setting multiple lines of type so that their baseline-to-baseline depth—or leading—is less than the point size of the type used. This is also known as minus line spacing. An example is setting 42-point type on 36-point leading.

Classifications
Typefaces are grouped into classifications according to design characteristics. The six classifications of

typefaces are: roman, sans serif, cursive, contemporary, italic, and text.

Columns

Large groups of text type all set in the same way, e.g., newspaper columns.

Continuous tone

A photograph or art that has shades of gray, i.e., not only black and white.

Copyfitting

Calculating length of text.

Counter

Enclosed, or partially enclosed white space within letters such as the top part of the *e* and bottom part of the *b*.

Crop marks

Lines on the outside corners of a page to mark the page's edges for trimming after it is printed.

DPI

Dots per inch.

Default

Preset condition of software.

Descender

Letters such as lowercase *g, p, q, y* which have portions that fall below the mass of the lowercase letters. The part that drops below the x-height is the descender.

Desktop publishing

Producing publication-quality documents from a microcomputer, page makeup software, and 300+ DPI printer.

Dingbats

Also known as pi characters, these are symbols such as arrows and boxes rather than letters.

Display advertisement

An advertisement within a publication that is set off by a border and usually has various sizes and styles of type.

Displaying type

The process of varying type's size, boldness, slant and arrangement based on the intended communication. Displaying emphasizes certain aspects of the presented information while playing down others. It visually organizes related items and funnels reader's attention through the message. Magazine and newspaper advertisements are examples of displaying type.

Display type	Large or prominent type, not text-size type.
Double truck	Advertisement that covers two facing pages and covers the inside page margins.
Em	Publishing industry unit of measure upon which wordspacing is based. The unit is as wide as the point size of type is high. It is the width of the capital M in most typefaces. For example, an em space in 10-point type is 10 points wide.
Em dash	A long dash the width of an em space. In typesetting, it's used in place of the typist's double hyphens.
En	One-half of an em space, or 50 percent of the point size of type used. Also known as a nut. The standard wordspacing for lines of all capital letters.
En dash	A dash the width of an en space. Used as a substitute for an em dash in large type sizes.
Face	The thick and thin strokes, dots and serifs that make up letters and other characters in typefaces. The part of type that prints.
Facing pages	The pairs of even and odd numbered pages that open up together, such as pages 2 and 3 in a publication. For design purposes facing pages are considered as one unit.
Family	A subunit of the classifications of type. A family of type is all the variations in design of a particular typeface. For example, Times, Times Bold, Times Italic and Times Bold Italic are all members of the same family. They share the same design characteristics, but differ in weight and slant.
Fill-in	When the white space between type or dots fills in during printing. Also called *plugging*.
Five-em	The width of one-fifth of an em space. 20 percent of

the width of the type being used. The minimum wordspacing to use in a justified line of type.

Flush left   See *Ragged right.*

Flush right   See *Ragged left.*

Font   One complete set of type characters, of one size, of one particular series, in a typeface family. In desktop publishing, *font* is a misnomer, it's used where *series* is meant.

Foot mark   A single straight mark (') indicating the preceding number is a measurement in feet. In typewriter style, an apostrophe and opening single quote.

Four-color process   Full color reproduction process that creates all necessary colors by using combinations of the three primary colors and black.

Four-em   The width of one-fourth of an em space. 25 percent of the width of the type being used. The same width as most punctuation. Also known as a thin space.

Frame   Box that surrounds a graph.

Golden proportion   3 to 5 proportion.

Grid lines   Background horizontal or vertical lines that mark numerical increments in bar or line graphs.

Gutter   The two inside page margins of facing pages combined.

Halftone   Continuous tone art that has been screened into a series of large and small dots for printing.

Hanging indention   A typesetting indention in which the first line of a paragraph is set to the full width and subsequent lines are all indented on the left by a uniform amount, commonly an em space.

Hard spacing   Invariable wordspacing.

Inch marks   Double straight marks (") indicating the preceding number is a measurement in inches, sometimes called *neutral quotes*. When using a typewriter, these are opening and closing quotes.

Ink	Pigments mixed with a vehicle, usually oil.

Justified type

Lines of type set so that all are spaced out to a common column width. Because each line has a different amount of space taken up in letters, the amount of wordspacing and letterspacing varies from line to line in justified type.

Kerning

Eliminating the excess built-in space between certain combinations of characters such as *LT* and *We*. It minimizes distracting white space gaps within words. Kerning function is also used to tighten up the letterspacing in lines of display type.

Layout

Drawing that shows the size and space relationships between elements in a page or an advertisement.

Leaders

Rows of periods used to lead the reader's eye across a column in tables of numbers.

Leaded type

Lines of type with two extra points of space between, such as 12-point type with 14-point leading.

Leading

The term used to refer to the amount of space between lines of type. Leading can be measured by the total distance from the baseline of one line of type to the baseline of the next. It can also be measured by the total distance from the top of the capitals of one line to the top of the capitals of the next. For instance, 10-point type with four extra points of space between each line is said to be 10-point type with 14-point leading.

Legend

Identifies each series in a graph.

Letterspacing

Extra spacing between letters.

Ligatures

Generally, two or more letters combined into one. Practically, ligatures refer to fl and fi combinations which, when made into ligatures become fl and fi.

The reason for ligatures is that the shape of the projecting top stroke of the lowercase *f* ends up on top of the upper part of the *l* and on top of the dot over the *i* when it's set immediately before either one of them without letterspacing.

Line	A horizontal sequence of words.
Line art	Art that is only black and white, i.e., has no shades of gray.
Line gauge	A measuring device marked in point and pica increments.
Lines per inch	Characteristic of a printed screen referring to its amount of dots per square inch. Screens are course or fine depending upon how many lines per square inch make them up. The more lines per inch a screen has, the smaller the dots are and the finer, or more capable of detail, the screen is.
Line space	Space between lines of type.
Logo	Logotype, an organization's unique identifying symbol.
Margin	The difference in size of the type page, or image on the page, and the paper page.
Measure	Width of a column of type.
Mechanical	A pasteup, or other camera-ready art.
Modern roman	A subunit of the roman typeface classification, modern roman typefaces have sharp, straight serifs that depart from their main strokes at a ninety degree angle, forming square corners. They have high contrast between thick and thin strokes and are crisp and finely detailed, with great clarity and legibility. Modern roman faces express mechanical precision, formality and authority rather than grace and friendliness. Their stroke orientation is mainly vertical.

Monospaced typefaces	Monospaced typefaces are typewriter-like typefaces. They allow the same amount of horizontal space for wide letters such as *w,* as they do for narrow letters such as *i.* This design characteristic creates wide gaps between many letters.
Neutral quotes	see *Foot mark.*
Newsprint	Absorbent, rough paper used to print newspapers.
Oldstyle roman	A subunit of the roman typeface classification, oldstyle typefaces are rounded at the serif and main stem junction, forming a curved wedge-like bracket. They generally have small contrast in the weight of their strokes—the body of the letters themselves are not very thick in some parts and very thin in others. Main stroke angles and the rounded serif bracket angles harmonize. Ascender stroke endings, like the top of the *l* and the top of the *h,* emulate the graceful angular cut of a letter drawn with a quill pen. They have an evenness of tone that does not dazzle the eye with contrasts. Because they generally have small x-heights, they don't require much extra leading as text.
Optical center	The spot at which the eye first rests when viewing a page. This is approximately 45 percent of the distance down from the top edge of the page and 55 percent of the distance up from the bottom edge.
Orphan	A short word, or short part of a word, that's left over at the end of a paragraph and comprises the entire last line of the paragraph. A reasonable guideline is to call any word of under five characters in such circumstances, an orphan.
Paper page	The size and shape of the document itself, as opposed to the type page which is the image that's to be printed on the paper page.
Paragraph space	Added space between paragraphs of text.

Paste-up	Camera-ready art and type positioned for reproduction, also known as a mechanical.
Pica	Increment of the publishing industry's system of measurement. It is 12 points wide or approximately one-sixth of an inch.
Points	Industry standard of measurement for type. It is about one seventy-second of an inch, or one-twelfth of one pica.
PostScript	Computer page description language for professional quality graphics.
Primary colors	Set of colors from which all others can be created. In printing they are cyan, magenta and yellow. Black is added in the four-color process to bring out image detail.
Printer's oblong	A proportion of 2 to 3.
Printing plate	Flexible image-carrying device that selectively attracts ink for image offset onto a press's blanket and transfer to paper.
Proportional typefaces	Typefaces designed so that the horizontal space an individual letter is allowed in a line varies in proportion to the width of the shape of the letter, e.g., an *m* is allowed more space than an *l*.
Pullout quotes	Phrases extracted from the text on a page and set in larger type. Also called *callouts*.
Ragged left	Lines of type that are set with invariable wordspacing, aligned on the right margin and uneven on the left margin. Also known as *flush right*.
Ragged right	Lines of type that are set with invariable wordspacing, aligned on the left margin and uneven on the right margin. Also known as *flush left*.
Reflective art	Art that is not transparent, i.e., not a film negative or film positive.

Register marks	Markings applied to camera-ready copy to align successive layers of colors.
Resolution	Relative precision with which art or letters are drawn. Determined in dots per inch (DPI).
Reverse	Coloring the background rather than the type or art on it.
Roman typefaces	Typefaces most obviously characterized by serifs. There are three kinds of roman typefaces: oldstyle, transitional and modern.
Rule	A horizontal or vertical drawn mark.
Sans serif typefaces	Typefaces with no serifs.
Series (graph)	Group of data.
Series (type)	All the variations in point size of a particular style in a typeface family. Times Bold, for instance, whether in 6 point or in 96 point, is a series in the Times family. In desktop publishing, a series is mislabeled *font*.
Serifs	The short lines stemming from the upper and lower ends of the main strokes of a letter. Their shapes can be hooks, blocks, or wedges and they terminate at an angle to the main strokes.
Set	The relative wideness or narrowness of the design of a typeface's characters.
Small caps	A type attribute that makes uppercase letters smaller than full-size capitals.
Specing type	Selecting size and style of type.
Subheads	Minor headlines.
Tabular matter	Information, primarily numerical, set into vertical columns for easy comprehension, i.e., newspaper stock market listings and baseball box scores.

Text	The main body of a printed page, not headlines, captions, large type, illustrations or photographs.
Three-em	The normal space between words. The name is a contraction for three-to-the-em, meaning there are three of them in each em. A three-em space is 33 percent of the point size of type being used. It is the optimum size of wordspacing to use between words set in lowercase or capital and lowercase letters.
Thumbnail sketch	Stage of the design process where layout ideas are drawn freehand. A rough sketch which includes all essential elements: type groups, headlines and artwork.
Tracking	Eliminating or adding a specified amount of letterspacing between each character.
Transitional typefaces	A subunit of the roman typeface classification, transitional typefaces have some aspects of both oldstyle and modern roman typefaces, bridging the two categories. Their serifs are less curved than are oldstyle faces and tend towards right angles and their strokes have more pronounced contrast between thick and thin. Transitional roman typefaces attempt to obtain the clarity of modern roman typefaces and the overall readable tone of oldstyle roman typefaces.
Transparency	Positive image on a transparent base. Used for projection.
Typeface	Type of a single design.
Type page	The image that's to be printed on the paper page; the mass of type and art on the paper page. For margin calculations the type page does not include the page number or a small footer or header.
Typographer	A specialist in the design, choice and arrangement of type matter.

Typographic color	The relative evenness and weight of strokes that make up a typeface. Also the relative evenness of the distribution of white space around the letters in a typeface. A type group's tone.
Typography	The study of type and its use. Also the style, arrangement or appearance of typeset matter.
Vertical justification	The process of aligning the top lines and bottom lines of multiple columns on a page, or of multiple pages, by spacing them all to the same depth.
White space	Area of design that has no text or graphics. Serves to punctuate art and display type and to divide and organize elements.
Widow	When the last typeset line of a paragraph is carried over on its own to the top of the following column or page. Standards vary, but it's reasonable to say that a full line—one that has enough words to fill out the entire line, even if it's the last line of a paragraph—is not a widow.
Word divisions	The division and hyphenation of a multi-syllable word at the end of a line on which the entire word will not fit.
Wordspacing	Spaces between words.
X-axis	Horizontal axis in a bar or line graph.
X-height	The mass of a lowercase letter, most easily measured by the height of the lowercase x in a typeface.
Y-axis	Vertical axis in a bar or line graph.

Index

About This Book

Typography for Desktop Publishers was produced on a Macintosh SE and a LaserWriter IINT. The camera-ready copy was runout on a Linotype Linotronic L-300 at 1,250 dots per inch.

The text was set and spell-checked in Microsoft Word 3.01. Grammar-checking was done with Lexpertise MacProof. Pages were made up in Aldus PageMaker 3.0. Illustrations were done in Page-Maker, MacPaint and Aldus Freehand.

Headlines are Bodoni and Bodoni Bold. Text is 10-point New Century Schoolbook on a leading of 13. Page numbers and chapter numbers are set in Poster Bodoni.